Search for the Serpent's Stone

Dan DeKoning

This book is a work of fiction. Names, characters, places, and incidents either are products of the author's imagination or are used fictitiously. Any resemblance to actual persons, living or dead, business establishments, events, or locales is entirely coincidental.

Copyright © 2025 by Dan DeKoning
All rights reserved. No part of this book may be reproduced or used in any manner without written permission of the copyright owner except for the use of quotations in a book review.

Cover Design by GetCovers

ISBN: 978-1-963691-09-2

DEDICATION

This book is dedicated to all the geocachers out there.
Hiders and Finders all.
See you on the trail!

Search for the Serpent's Stone

CHAPTER ONE

"Are you sure the cache is under here?" Drake Decker called from under the bridge that spanned a six-foot-wide creek.

"I'm pretty sure. Keep looking," Allie Ashe answered as she inspected the steel handrail that ran the entire span at hip level. Allie spotted a pair of joggers coming her way on the walking path, so she moved to the middle of the bridge, placed her arms nonchalantly on the rail, and gazed at the running water.

"There are muggles coming," Allie said, to alert Drake that there were people in the area who didn't know about geocaching.

The joggers slowed and came to a stop a few feet before the bridge deck.

"Is everything okay here?" one of the joggers asked.

Allie looked over and surveyed the pair. Two women, both brunettes, wearing similar outfits consisting of black leggings and sports bras. The woman on the left wore a teal bra, the woman on the right, who asked Allie the question, wore a baby blue one.

"I'm sorry?" Allie asked.

"There's a man under the bridge," the woman said. "Is there

something wrong with it?"

Allie recognized the women had busted them, so she decided that honesty was the best policy. "No. There's nothing wrong with the bridge. My friend and I are geocaching. We're trying to find something someone else hid, kind of like a scavenger hunt."

"Ah, gotcha," the woman said. "What are you looking for?"

"I don't know for sure. That's part of the fun. The container could be anything that could hold a piece of paper. A prescription bottle, a small box, a film cannister. Anything, really."

"Oh. Okay. Well, you have fun with that," the woman said. "Come on."

The woman and her friend began to walk across the bridge. When they got halfway and were about to pass Allie, the woman turned and winked at her. "You're pretty close to the cache where you are. The container is a fake nut." The woman smiled and she and her friend jogged away.

Allie turned her attention toward the river and looked over the edge of the rail. Every six inches was a horizontal metal brace, secured by nuts and bolts, that ran from the top of the handrail to the bridge deck.

From where she stood, Allie began examining each nut and bolt by hand, checking to discover if she could turn them with her fingers. She tried a dozen bolts in order before turning around and making her way back toward the other end of the bridge. Rather than skip all the nuts she just tried, she tried them all again, in case she'd missed one.

"Ow!" Drake yelled from below.

Allie leaned farther over the bridge, but she couldn't see her best friend and geocaching partner. "What was that?"

"I hit my head on a support beam," Drake said. "Are you sure this stupid thing is down here? I see nothing except dirt and spiderwebs."

"Keep looking. Someone found this bugger yesterday, so it

must be here somewhere."

Allie made it past where she started and four bolts later, using only her fingers, a nut turned easily. She looked over the edge and realized she should have noticed it right away, since the bolt she had her hand on was the only one that had two nuts on the bolt. Careful not to drop the container, Allie unscrewed the nut. When she got it into her hand, she recognized it as a less-common hiding method, but one she'd encountered plenty of times before. One end of the nut was still usable and screwed onto the end of a bolt. The other end of the nut had a hollowed-out piece of bolt welded to the nut, making it look like the bolt continued through it. The hollowed-out space usually contained the log, but Allie couldn't get it out. She checked her pocket for tweezers and realized she'd lent it to Drake on the previous cache.

"Marco!" Allie yelled. It was their way of letting each other know that one of them had found the geocache.

"Polo! On the way," Drake said.

Allie turned around and watched as Drake's head appeared over the bridge deck as he climbed up the embankment to level ground.

When he approached, Allie had him turn in a slow circle as she brushed the spiderwebs and dirt from his five-seven frame. He stopped for a moment, removed his Tennessee Titans baseball cap, then ran his fingers through his short blond hair.

"Do you see any spiders?" Drake asked, bending over so Allie could see the top of his head.

Allie ran her fingers through his hair.

"Wait! Stand still!"

Drake imitated a statue. Allie moved in closer and slowly pinched his ear.

"Got it!"

Drake backed away and started rubbing his head. "Funny, Allie cat. Funny. You got the cache?"

Allie held up the nut. "I need my tweezers, though."

"It's in your pouch," Drake said.

"The pouch in your pocket?" Allie asked.

Drake patted the front pockets of his jeans, found Allie's pouch, and handed it to her. Allie took the blue pouch, opened it and removed the tweezers. After handing the pouch back to Drake, she tipped the bolt upside-down and tried to coax the paper log out from inside.

"Is there a paper clip in there?" Allie asked.

Drake opened the pouch, dug around it in for a moment, and extracted a paper clip. He held it out, and Allie traded it for the tweezers.

Allie bent the end of the paper clip so it was straight and inserted it into the bolt. She gave it a couple of pokes, turned the bolt upside-down, and the small paper log dropped into her open palm. She returned the paper clip to the pouch, tucked the bolt into her jeans pocket, and unrolled the tiny slip of paper. Allie wore her long red hair in a ponytail and tucked behind her ear was a pen, which she used to put her geocaching nickname on the log. When she finished, she handed the paper and pen to Drake, who added his name under hers. While Drake rolled up the log, Allie fished the bolt from her pocket. She took the paper from him, placed it back in the bolt, and returned the nut to where she found it.

"There. Another one done," Allie said.

"Where's the next?"

Allie dug her phone out of her pocket and opened her favorite geocaching app. She looked at the map, then pointed to the north.

"That way."

Together, the pair walked across the bridge and along the path. Fifty yards ahead of them was a park bench, and when they got near, Drake pointed at the bench and they both sat. Drake kicked off his left shoe. He picked it off the ground and ran his fingers around the inside.

"Have you heard from Geneva lately?" Allie asked.

"Lately, as in like, within the last two hours that I've been with you?"

Allie smiled.

"I talked to her this morning. We talk almost every morning. It's the highlight of my day."

"When did you become such a romantic?" Allie asked.

Drake feigned a shocked look. "Geneva says I'm the most romantic man she's ever been involved with."

Allie laughed. "Geneva told me about the men she's dated in the past. You're just the first one who walks without dragging his knuckles on the ground."

Drake playfully hit his friend on the shoulder. "Not nice, Allie."

"So, spill the beans. When is the big wedding? Where's it going to be? Am I going to be your best man?"

"Hold on. Pump the brakes a bit."

"Wait, you tell me I got to witness that romantic proposal in Italy, and you want to hit the brakes on the wedding?"

"We've decided on a long engagement."

"What? Why? You two are perfect for each other."

"I agree, but we live half a country apart. I'm here in Nashville, she's in Boston. It would be one thing if she had a job she could easily quit, but..."

"But being a symphony conductor is her dream. I get it, Drake. It's hard to give up on something like that."

"I know. She says the wedding is on just as soon as her current contract runs out. That's two years? Three years? I'm not quite sure."

"Why don't you simply move out there?" Allie asked. "There's not a whole lot tying you down here."

"My parents are here."

"So what? You've got plenty of money to take them out to

Boston, too. Buy them a nice little house. Take your dad to Red Sox games, eat lots of chowder."

Drake chuckled. "That's pronounced chow-dah, I believe. Like I'd be able to get my dad off of his multi-generational farm and drop him down in the big city. He'd be miserable."

"You mean that you would be miserable. You hated our trip out there."

"Not all of it. I enjoyed hanging out with you, and Ingrid, and Geneva."

"Me too," Allie said.

"Oh, and the history was cool, too." Drake said. He bent over and banged his sneaker upside-down. On the third hit, a chunk of mulch flew out and came to rest in the middle of the walking path.

"I agree," Allie said. "I could've done without the kidnappings and all the injuries."

"Same, same," Drake said.

They fell silent for a moment while Drake put his shoe back on. When he finished, he turned to Allie with a giant smile on his face.

"Finding that treasure was great, too."

Allie's eyebrows raised as she nodded. "That wasn't the worst thing to ever happen to us."

Without asking, Drake rose from the bench and started up the path. Allie got to his side a few seconds later.

"Still north?" Drake asked.

Allie checked her app, then veered off to the east. "Head for those trees over there."

The pair left the pavement and cut across a patch of grass thirty yards wide, headed for a row of trees that designated the greenway boundary. It took only a handful of minutes to meander across the grass.

"Is there a hint with this one?" Drake asked

Allie checked her app. "Just hanging around."

Drake nodded. "Well, that's better than nothing, I guess."

Drake and Allie each picked a different tree and started searching the branches.

"Marco!" Drake called.

"Polo! That was fast," Allie said, stepping over to join her friend.

"It's not too hard to find a pine cone in a maple tree," Drake said, holding the geocache up by its hanger. Dangling from his fingers was a plastic pine cone with a small bison tube embedded in it. Once used primarily to hold pills, the bison had become a popular geocaching container.

While Drake unscrewed the tube and retrieved the log inside, Allie got her pen ready to ink her name.

"Here," Drake said, handing her the log.

Allie added her name, passed the pen and log to Drake, then stepped back out into the grass as she waited for Drake to place the cache back where he got it from. While she was waiting, she logged her find in the app and located the next nearest geocache. It appeared to be only a tenth of a mile up the greenway.

Drake stepped out of the trees and followed Allie's lead as she headed back to the path.

"How's Ingrid?" Drake asked.

"Still in Denmark."

"She's been there a while, hasn't she?"

"Over a month," Allie said. "Another week and she'll be back in Boston."

"Why didn't you go with her?"

"We talked about it. She and her folks went to a wedding and family reunion thing. I thought it would be awkward to spend six weeks with people I've never met before. We're thinking about a trip to Denmark in the summer."

"Mind if Geneva and I tag along for that one?" Drake asked.

Allie didn't have to think too long for the answer to that particular question. Drake had been her best geocaching friend for years, and since they'd met Geneva and Ingrid, best friends from Boston, at a geocaching competition a couple of years before, they'd all been inseparable as a group.

"Well, Ingrid and I will have to talk it over, but I'm sure it might be okay. We enjoy having Geneva around."

Drake stopped, put his hands on his hips, and leaned forward slightly. "Geneva? What about me?"

Allie turned and saw Drake looking ridiculous in his current pose. She stepped over and put her hand lovingly on Drake's cheek. "Of course we want you there, too." She patted his cheek and smiled. "Someone needs to haul all the luggage."

Drake let his jaw drop, and Allie laughed. He did his best to look dejected and hurt, but that just made Allie laugh harder. She grabbed him by the hand and gave him a tug to get him moving again.

Allie led Drake down the path, and they soon came to another bench.

"It should be there," Allie said, motioning to the green metal seat.

"You want to search the top or bottom?" Drake said.

"Top. I did bottom last time."

Allie heard a ding from her phone and switched from her geocaching app to her email while Drake positioned himself behind the bench, dropped to his knees, and began searching under the seat for the cache container.

Allie read through the email she'd just received, then sat on the bench and read it again.

"Hey, you're blocking my light," Drake said.

"Forget that a moment. Come up here."

Drake found his feet and slid into the seat next to Allie. "What's up?"

"I just got this really fascinating email."

"Let me guess, it's from some geocaching group that wants you to come and appear at some event or whatever."

"Why would you guess that?" Allie asked.

Drake took his cap from his head, placed it on his knee, and ran his hand through his hair. "Because it's not unusual. I get emails like that all the time. So does Geneva. We've actually started comparing them to see which request is the most ridiculous. Since we found those treasures in Boston and Italy, we've been in enough news articles to draw interest from every geocacher and random treasure hunter across the country. I must get invitations to ten different events a week."

"This one's not from around here, though. Listen to this. Dear Ms. Ashe. I am writing to invite you to the first ever Australian Outback Geocaching Invitational. At this event, select teams from around the world will compete in a geocaching event greater than any contest ever held before. The winner will receive ten-thousand American dollars, along with a secret grand prize, which will be a valuable Australian artifact with great historical significance."

"Ten grand?" Drake said. "That's what? A week's worth of interest from the bank? Besides, it would cost us more in plane tickets to get there."

"But wait, there's more," Allie said.

Drake sighed. "There usually is."

"According to the email, they will cover the cost of plane tickets and accommodations for up to four people on a team. Even if we didn't win, it would be a free trip for us to Australia. I've always wanted to go to Australia. Haven't you, Drake?"

Drake shrugged, then put his hat on. "I never really thought about it one way or the other."

"Oh, come on, you stick in the mud. It'll be fun. They have kangaroos and koala bears down there. So cute!"

"Don't they also have alligators, snakes, spiders, lizards, and all kinds of other things that will kill you just by looking at it wrong?"

Allie sighed. "They don't have alligators. They have

crocodiles."

"What's the difference?" Drake asked.

Allie grinned. "One you see later, one you see after a while." After she got the words out, Allie started laughing.

"Funny, Allie. How long have you been waiting to slip that one into random conversation?"

Allie shrugged. "I don't know. Twenty-five years, maybe?"

"Was it worth it?" Drake asked.

Allie grinned. "Oh, yes. It was quite satisfying. Seriously, though, I doubt they'd put on an event where anyone would be in any real danger."

"Don't you remember when you tore your knee apart in Arizona a few years ago? Or when I fell off the side of that mountain in Italy? Or when Ingrid got shot in Boston?"

"Well, technically, we weren't geocaching when Ingrid got shot," Allie said.

"You know what I mean. It's geocaching. An outdoor activity, and anything can happen outdoors. How many times have we gotten stung by bees, or scared by snakes, or poked with thorns, or almost fell into rivers, or turned an ankle, or any other of a random number of injuries and accidents?"

"Not today," Allie said. "Neither one of us."

Drake rolled his eyes. "The day is still early yet."

"Drake Decker, are you trying to be a party pooper? Like I said, even if we don't win, we'll have a great time. Free vacation, Drake. Free."

"It seems free always comes with some cost, Allie. Remember, in St. Thomas we got roped into that three-hour sales pitch for a timeshare that neither one of us wanted, just for a free bottle of rum that was so small it only made us two drinks?"

"Oh, come on, Drake. We were staying at an all-inclusive place, anyway. You had access to all the booze you wanted." Drake leaned forward, put his elbows on his knees, and dropped his chin to his chest.

"Come on, Drake. I don't see a downside here. We already have our passports, and they'll pay for the trip. You know, the email said a team of up to four, so I could just take Geneva and Ingrid with me and leave your sorry butt behind. I'm sure you have plenty of other things to do, like watching sports, eating sandwiches while standing over your sink, and missing the three of us while you were wishing you were along for the ride."

"What's the date of the contest?"

Allie read through the email, found the info, and passed it on. "Ingrid will be back from Denmark by then. I'll have to check with Geneva to see if that interferes with the symphony season."

"Well, you drive a hard bargain," Drake said.

"So, you'll go?" Allie asked.

Drake looked down, and on the corner of the bench, spotted a pocket cache that used a magnet to attach itself to the seat. He freed it and passed it to Allie. "Why not? You know I love finding geocaches."

CHAPTER TWO

"Where are they?" Allie asked. As she sat in the chair at the gate, she subconsciously began bouncing her right leg up and down like she was keeping beat to a heavy metal song playing in her head.

"Relax," Drake said. "They'll be here. We've got a good two hours before this flight leaves. That gives them plenty of time."

"Yeah, but you know how I am. Two hours early is still late." Allie got to her feet, found her five-foot-six self wasn't tall enough to see over the men milling about, so she moved to one side to peek down the hall.

"Relax, will you?"

Down the corridor, Allie spotted a blond woman headed in her direction. She put her hand in the air and started to wave, but dropped her arm when the woman turned right and sat down at the gate for the flight headed to London.

"Crap. Not her," Allie said.

"Can you watch my bag? I'm going to run down and get a coffee," Drake said, directing Allie back to her chair. He put his luggage on the seat next to Allie to save it for himself.

"Can you get me one? I'd love a mocha latte." Allie said.

Drake smiled. "No way. You're too high-strung as it is. I'll compromise with you, though, and get you a bottle of water."

Allie frowned, but didn't say anything. From her backpack, she extracted a small tablet, powered it up, and selected one of the ten books she had downloaded for the long flights there and back, as well as the time she'd spend at night under the southern sky reading and relaxing. She tried to focus on the words, couldn't with all the noise at the gate, and popped her headphones into the tablet and pressed the button to have the app read it aloud to her.

With the voice droning on in her ears, Allie closed her eyes, breathed deep a few times, and finally started to relax. After ten minutes, she felt herself slipping into that state where she wasn't quite asleep, yet wasn't quite awake, either. She sensed someone get close, then a hand fell on her shoulder.

She opened her eyes, expecting to see Drake holding out a bottle of water for her. Instead, she gazed into the prettiest ice-blue eyes she'd ever seen. A smile instantly spawned on each woman's face, and Ingrid leaned in for a hug.

"You're here!" Allie exclaimed.

Ingrid pulled away from the hug, slipped her backpack from her shoulders, and placed it on the floor in front of Drake's chair. She set Drake's bag next to hers, and sat, taking Allie's hand in hers.

"I hear you've been waiting not-so-patiently for me," Ingrid said.

"From?"

"Drake. We spotted him at the coffee shop. Geneva is in line there with him."

Allie didn't speak. Instead, she just stared at her friend. There was no hiding the Scandinavian look in Ingrid Snyder. Besides her ice-blue eyes, she had long blond, almost white, hair, and alabaster skin. She didn't have a mark on her perfect body, other than a star-shaped scar on her side where she'd taken a bullet, and a white streak on her leg from where she'd almost slid down a mountain in the Alps.

"How was Denmark?" Allie asked.

"Good. You should have been there with me. Everyone would have loved you."

"I don't think my Danish would be strong enough to meet your family over there."

"What have you learned so far?" Ingrid asked.

"*Hej*," Allie said, pronouncing it as 'hedge'.

"Impressive," Ingrid said, "but if you're trying to say hello to me, it's pronounced like 'hi' in English."

"Just hi?" Allie asked.

Ingrid nodded. "Yes. But I'm so pleased with your progress. We'll be holding secret conversations between us in Danish in no time."

"What do you plan on talking about?" Geneva Benson asked as she approached Allie. She bent over and gave Allie a hug. Geneva was the only brunette of the group, and unlike Allie and Ingrid, she wore her hair short. Her hazel eyes cast a continuous sparkle, helped by the flecks of gold and green within them. Her haircut worked perfectly with her round face, and she had a button nose and natural lips.

Ingrid gave her a sly smile. "Why, you and Drake, of course. It would be rude to talk about you behind your backs in English."

Ingrid gave a titter, and Allie joined in.

The area quieted down as the Qantas personnel began making boarding announcements.

"We'll be up soon," Allie said. "Then it's only a short, seventeen-hour jaunt to Sydney."

* * *

An exhausted Allie sighed, which turned into a yawn so wide it made her head shake. Although she'd done her best to sleep during the long flight, at most she'd gotten only a handful of hours in. She'd spent most of the time reading and watching movies on the entertainment system built into the seat in front of her. Once the sun came up, she leaned against the bulkhead and stared at the blue waters of the southern Pacific. A moment later, land came into view, and the plane started its descent.

Allie watched as the ground rose to greet her. The Sydney skyline grew bigger, and she watched the traffic on the roads below her. The sights lulled her off to sleep, and she jerked awake a few minutes later when the plane's wheels contacted the runaway.

She glanced to her left and noticed Ingrid looking past her and out her window.

"We've made it," Ingrid said. "Finally."

Allie blinked a few times to clear the cobwebs from her head, then looked at her friend. "I thought you would be used to the long flights going to and from Copenhagen all the time."

Ingrid shook her head. "No. I can fly there and back in less time than this flight. I can't wait to get off this plane."

An hour later, the group got out of a cab and walked through the front doors of the Amaroo Inn. Although the skyscrapers surrounded the boutique hotel and it was only a few blocks from the famed Sydney Harbor, stepping into the lobby seemed like traipsing into a jungle scene. Bamboo lined the walls on either side of the corridor leading to the front desk. Along the walls stood planters with a dazzling display of purple flowers. Each delicate flower had exactly five petals that fanned out in a semi-circle. Allie stopped, bent over, and inhaled deeply. The light, sweet scent of the blooms brought a smile to her face. She stood and approached the front desk.

"Good morning," the desk agent said, a smile on his face as fresh as the new day. He wore khaki pants and a shirt that reminded Allie more of Hawaii than Australia. According to his name tag, his name was Steve.

"Good morning. I'm Alyssa Ashe. I should have a reservation for two rooms."

Steve clicked a few keys on the computer and brought up her information. "Yes. Two rooms. The bad news is check-in isn't until three. Normally, I'd put you up in other rooms, but I have none available."

"What time is it now?" Allie asked.

Steve smiled. "Just after nine a.m."

Allie shrugged. "I guess we're a little early."

"No worries, it happens all the time with flights from the States. If you want to wait, there's a coffee shop two doors down from here. Or, if you'd like to explore the city for a few hours, there are many attractions within a short walk from here."

"What about…"

Allie stopped when Steve held up his hand, expecting her next question. "You can drop your luggage here. I'll put it in the locked luggage room, and it will be safe and sound until your return. If you give me your cell number, I will call you as soon as your rooms are ready."

"I'll be back in a moment." Allie turned around and addressed her friends. "Bad news. We can't have rooms for another six hours."

"What are we supposed to do?" Drake asked.

"He says there's a coffee shop nearby, or we can see the sites for a few hours," Allie said.

Geneva turned her phone around and pointed. "There are plenty of geocaches over in this enormous park a few blocks to the east. Why not go there?"

Steve cleared his throat, and everyone turned to look at him. "That would be the Royal Botanic Gardens. Quite a great place to spend some time. South of that is Hyde Park, which is also quite lovely. I believe that's where the other group went."

"What other group?" Allie asked.

"Four others came in about an hour ago. They were from Germany, or Belgium. Somewhere around there. They headed off to the park, too."

"What makes you think we're part of the same group?" Drake asked.

"Invoice on the reservations. They're both going to some outback geo-what's-its association."

Drake nodded. "Are you expecting anyone else from our group, or has anyone else already checked in?"

"No, mate. Only the eight of you. Like I said, they went to the park. If you're lucky, you might run into them there."

"Why lucky?" Drake asked.

"It's an enormous park."

"Well, Steve," Allie said, "I guess you sold it to us. Where should we put our luggage?"

Steve came around the desk, put tags around the handles of the bags staying behind, tore off the claim checks, and handed them to Allie. The group waited until Steve loaded the luggage onto a cart and wheeled it into a nearby room before they turned and left the hotel.

Once out on the sidewalk, Geneva glanced at her app and pointed toward the east. "That way," she said. She held out her hand and flexed it a few times, signaling to Drake that he should take it. Once he did, Geneva led him toward the park, with Allie and Ingrid falling a few steps behind them. They strolled leisurely down Bridge Street. When they reached the Museum of Sydney, Drake spotted a half-wall in front of the building and made a beeline for it. When he reached it, he sat, expelling a loud exhale as he did.

"Don't tell me you're already tired," Geneva said.

"I've been tired. I've never been in need of a nap as much as I am right now."

Geneva pulled at his arm. "Come on, lazy man. I can see the

park from here. Another couple of blocks and we'll find you a nice bench to collapse into. Or you can lie under a tree and take a nap."

"Argh," Drake moaned as Geneva dragged him to his feet.

"Come on, Drake," Geneva said as she urged him on.

Two blocks later, they all crossed the street and found themselves standing in front of a building that resembled a white castle, complete with battlements on the towers and walls.

"Conservatorium of Music. 1915," Drake said, reading the name on the building. "Where to from here, Geneva?"

Geneva took a moment to check her app. "Well, we have a choice. There are half a dozen caches to the south, and about the same to the north."

"Which way is north?" Drake asked.

Geneva pointed to her left. "That way about four-tenths of a mile. Toward the opera house."

"The Sydney Opera House?" Ingrid asked. "I've always wanted to see that. Let's go that way."

Without waiting for a response, Ingrid grabbed Allie by the hand, gave her a tug, and they walked north, with Geneva and Drake following behind. The group marched in silence for ten minutes, following the pedestrian path through the park. Up ahead, the opera house grew larger with every step they took.

"I'm guessing the geocache is at that tree," Allie said, pointing a hundred feet ahead of them. "And I think we found the Germans as well."

The park seemed crowded with perhaps two-dozen people in all. Most were tourists, focused on the opera house and taking pictures of that and the Sydney Harbor Bridge across the bay. A few joggers were doing laps around the park, and there was a small group of five in the middle of a downward dog yoga position. Only four people in the park looked suspicious enough to be geocachers, and they were the ones interested in a tree and not the surrounding scenery.

"I guess so," Drake said. "Let's go say hello."

The group began walking toward the tree and had closed half of the distance when one of the geocachers at the tree noticed them. The man stood straight and patted the person next to him on the shoulder. Soon, all four, three men and one woman, noticed the group approaching, and rather than stick around, they left the tree at a fast walk, followed a wrought-iron fence until they came to a gate, then left the park and went off in the direction of the opera house.

"That wasn't friendly," Ingrid said.

"Not at all," Drake said.

Geneva was the first one to reach the tree, and since the nearest branch was fifteen feet above them, it took only a cursory search of the trunk for her to find the cache container, which turned out to be a black plastic film canister. Geneva opened up the cap and pulled from the can a small plastic bag, in which was the paper log. She signed the log, then passed it to everyone in the group before putting everything back together and placing the can where she found it. She logged the geocache on her app, then looked for the next closest one.

"There's a virtual next to the opera house," she announced.

The park was on a ridge with a fifteen-foot drop to the ground where the opera house stood. The friends followed the same path the Germans had, and when they exited the gate, they found themselves at the top of a stone staircase. Once they descended, they stood only a few hundred yards from the historic building.

The Sydney Opera House, being one of the most iconic buildings in the world, stopped all four friends in their tracks as they took in the view. The design featured sail-like shells, which resembled large white sails or waves clustered together.

"It's beautiful," Geneva said, the first one to speak.

"Of course it is. The architect was Danish," Ingrid said.

"Where's the cache?" Drake asked as he impatiently shifted

from foot to foot.

Geneva referenced the app. "It's a virtual. According to the description, we need to gather information from some historical plaques around here, and submit a picture of us when we upload the log."

"Okay, what do we need?" Allie asked.

Geneva took them to the first waypoint, which consisted of a plaque that contained information on the construction of the building. As they stood in the front of the plaque, Geneva read the cache description aloud, telling the group what question they needed to answer.

As Geneva and Allie read the plaque, Ingrid looked around the area.

"Hey, where's Drake?" Ingrid asked.

Allie spun around to look, but Geneva remained focused on the plaque. She began counting words, looking for the specific one she needed.

"I don't see him," Allie said.

"Did you look for the nearest bench?" Geneva asked.

Allie looked around the immediate area, but didn't see any bench in sight. She walked halfway back to where they started and spotted Drake. Not only had he found himself on a bench, but he laid down horizontal on it, his Titans baseball cap covering his face. She shrugged, then rejoined her friends.

"You're right, Geneva. He found a place to rest. If the wind blew in the right direction, we could probably hear him snoring from here," Allie said.

Geneva and Ingrid laughed.

"I got this answer. Let's move on," Geneva said.

Geneva led the women over to the next plaque, read the cache description, and started the hunt for the information they needed. Ingrid spotted the answer first, so Geneva jotted it down and led them to the other side of the opera house. There, they found a large group of people assembled for a tour, so they stood off to the side and out of the way and waited for the tour to enter the building.

While they waited, Allie leaned over a black steel rail and stared out at the waters lapping across the bay. From the docks nearby, she heard a horn blow and a few minutes later, a ferry came into view and started on a journey to the other side of the harbor. She'd half-looked at a ferry map before they'd left home, but since there were over two dozen places it could go, Allie didn't venture a guess as to where it was headed.

"What are you thinking?" Ingrid asked as she looped her arm through Allie's.

"Just wondering where that boat is going," Allie said as the ferry passed in front of them.

"My guess is that it's headed to the zoo," Ingrid said.

"The zoo?"

"Yeah. It's over there." Ingrid counted off the points of land she could see and gestured at the fourth one. "See where I'm pointing? It's right there."

"How can you tell?" Allie asked.

"I can see a giraffe. They're tall, you know," Ingrid teased.

Allie smiled and took Ingrid's hand in hers. "It's beautiful here, isn't it?"

Ingrid looked out over the water. "It's not Denmark, but it's okay. A little crowded for my taste, but nice."

Allie looked out across the water. In addition to the ferries, there were pleasure boats, charter boats, and a helicopter whirring across the bay. Way off in the distance, she spotted a large cruise ship slowly making its way in to the port. She understood Ingrid's comment without question.

As they both looked over the bay, Geneva came to Allie's other side and leaned over the rail just like Allie was doing.

"Get the last answer?" Allie asked without looking at her friend.

"Yep," Geneva said. "All we need now is take our picture

with the opera house, and we'll be good to go."

"Should we include Drake in it?" Allie asked.

Geneva grinned. "We could get him napping on the bench. That would probably make for an interesting selfie."

"Then what should we do?" Ingrid asked. "Find more geocaches?"

"I think we should kick Drake off the bench," Allie said.

"Why?" Geneva asked.

"I could use a nap myself."

CHAPTER THREE

"What are you looking at?" Ingrid asked Allie, who had an elbow on the armrest and her chin resting on her fist.

"Literally nothing. I'd heard the center of the country was desolate, but that was an understatement. I haven't seen so much as a road in the last thirty minutes."

Ingrid leaned closer to Allie and looked out of the plane window. All she spotted below was the earth in varying shades of reds, oranges, and browns. No vegetation, lakes, or rivers. No buildings, houses, or ranches, and the only things that passed for roads were paths of straight lines in the dirt. Ingrid moved back into her own space, took Allie's hand, and closed her eyes.

"I wish we would have had more time in Sydney," Ingrid said. "We've hardly done anything, and I'm already worn out."

Allie stayed silent but agreed. They'd spent only two days in Sydney, and after the long flight from Dallas and the walk to and from the Sydney Opera House, everyone in the group, including Drake who had gotten a nice nap in, were so exhausted that when they finally got room keys, they all turned in without so much as a conversation as when to meet up for dinner. Ingrid had woken

Allie a few minutes after eight. They tried rapping on Drake and Geneva's door, but no one answered, so Allie and Ingrid found a fast-food burger to squash the hunger pangs enough to carry them through to the morning.

The following day, the foursome broke into two couples. While Allie and Ingrid took the ferry across the bay to visit the Toranga Zoo, Drake and Geneva walked around downtown, window shopping and visiting random sites as they came across them. After another exhaustive day, the four met up for dinner before turning into bed early.

This morning, they found themselves on a flight to Alice Springs, which was a remote town in the heart of Australia's Northern Territory. The sleepy city of twenty-five thousand people sat almost at the geographical center of the country and was a common starting point for tourists wanting to explore the vast Outback.

Allie sat straight up when the scenery suddenly changed and the endless red dirt got replaced with views of the city with its structured blocks of houses, the greenery of parks scattered through the area, and more cars in one store parking lot than she'd seen over the previous two hours. The pilot made an announcement, and the plane began its descent to one of the two airport runways.

The group found a transport van waiting for them when they stepped out of the terminal, and after a fifteen minute drive, they got dropped off in front of a hotel where the staff met them at the front door. A bellhop collected their luggage and ushered them right into a large conference room. The conference room was set up banquet style, with four large, round tables with room for eight people at each. An elevated platform stood at one end of the room, on which sat a lectern with a microphone. Behind the lectern, the country flags of the United States, Canada, Germany, and Great Britain stood tall in stands, flanked by the national flag of Australia on either end.

Three of the tables had people sitting at them, and each had a man standing near them, all in conversation.

"G'day," a man said as he approached Allie and her friends, extending his hand. "I'm Zeke Miller, one of the hosts for this event. You must be the Americans." Zeke was tall and broad-shouldered. He wore his long black hair tied back, and his warm eyes sparkled as he smiled.

"Allie Ashe," she said, taking his hand. "How did you know we were American?"

Zeke broke the handshake and pointed at Drake's cap. "The hat. Broncos are popular down here. Sometimes you'll notice some Steelers, Cowboys, or Packers apparel, but you rarely see a Titans fan down here."

"Broncos, huh?" Drake said.

"Yeah, mate. I think it has more to do with the horse than the team. Anyway, welcome to Alice Springs. You're the fourth team to arrive. The other three teams should be here shortly."

"Only seven teams?" Drake asked.

"Yeah. Bloke from the French team broke his leg a few days ago, so they had to back out. Makes better odds for you, though, right? You're welcome to take that empty table and wait, or join one of the other groups." Zeke gave a half-wave and wandered away to join another table.

"Well, team," Allie said, "should we join another group, or be anti-social?"

"I vote for anti-social," Drake said. "In fact, I'm curious when our rooms will be available. I assume we're staying in this hotel?"

Allie was about to answer, but Drake held up a hand to interrupt her. "I'll go find out for myself."

Drake exhaled, then rose and left the conference room in a hurry.

"What's got his goat?" Allie asked as the three women wandered over to the empty table and took seats.

Geneva shrugged. "I think he's tired."

"Tired as in lack of sleep, or tired of this trip already?" Allie asked.

"A little of both, maybe," Geneva said. "He hasn't been sleeping well since we left the states. I think he's having difficulty adjusting to the time difference."

"Perhaps I shouldn't have talked him into coming on this trip. We could have made it a girl's trip and left him at home where he'd be much happier."

Geneva threw off the comment with a wave of her hand. "Come on, Allie. You've known him forever and know as well as I do that he'll come around."

Allie nodded. "You're probably right. Heads up. We've got incoming."

"You mind if we sit down?" a petite woman with long, sleek black hair and dark eyes asked.

Allie raised an eyebrow. "You're from the states?"

The woman reached out her hand. "Madison Turner. The boys are Jason Miller and Caleb Johnson. We're from Los Angeles."

"Please join us. I'm Allie Ashe. That's Geneva Benson, and the blond is Ingrid Snyder. I'm from Nashville. Those two are from Boston."

"You're the famous Allie Cat, aren't you?" Jason asked.

Allie's gaze moved to the man speaking to her. Jason was tall and athletic with short brown hair, a square jaw, and a firefighter's build. His tinted glasses made it hard for Allie to tell his eye color.

"How did you guess?"

"I saw you on that geocaching podcast a couple of months ago."

"And you remembered me? I'm flattered."

"I never forget a pretty face." Jason threw her a smile that Ingrid intercepted with a glare of her own.

Allie put a gentle hand on Ingrid's arm. "Flattery, Mr. Jason, won't get you anywhere with me."

Madison tugged on Jason's arm, forcing him to take a seat next to her. "Don't mind him. He's just your typical knuckle-dragging male."

Caleb took the seat on the other side of Madison, and the Americans struggled to make small talk with each other. As they passed the time, they didn't notice that the other two groups entered the room, with Drake bringing up the rear. When he joined his friends, he passed room keys to everyone. As they settled in, Zeke took a position behind the lectern and tapped on the microphone to see if it worked.

"G'day everyone. For those of you who I haven't met, my name is Zeke Miller. I'm part of the group putting on this exclusive event. The rest of the team is Aaron Davis. You can call him Aussie. Jake Thompson, and Ben McAllister."

As Zeke made the introductions, the men stood and raised a hand.

"Like the invitation said, this is a select group of geocachers who we invited to compete." He shuffled through a couple of sheets of paper on the lectern. "As I read through the list, stand up so everyone can see who you are. First up, from Germany, we have Anna Vogel, Klaus Berger, Jonas Weber, and Felix Schneider."

As each person stood, Allie studied them intently.

"I think those were the people who ran away from us at the opera house," Ingrid whispered to Allie.

"Yeah, I believe you're right," Allie responded. Since Ingrid had distracted her, she missed the names of the Canadians completely, and half of an Australian team. She almost missed her own introduction, but Ingrid elbowed her in the ribs when Allie's name was called. Allie stood, waited for the rest of her team to be called, then sat.

In short order, Zeke introduced the other American group,

the second Australian group, and the team from Great Britain, which was the only team consisting of two married couples. Once the Brits sat, Zeke called Aussie to the lectern.

"Hey," Aussie began, then stepped backward when the microphone gave off a squelch of feedback. While he waited for the sound to fade, he ran his fingers through his short, curly brown hair. Once it cleared, he slowly approached the mic and didn't lean in as far when he spoke. "Let's try this again. My name is Aussie. I'm a tour guide and have lived here in Alice Springs my entire life. In additional to cultural tours, I also take many groups out on geocaching adventures, so I'm the one who designed the caches you'll be out there finding. In essence, you'll be going one multi-cache with many steps to it. You'll get the starting coordinates before you leave this room today. Then it's up to you how you want to go after this."

The Germans at the front table started speaking animatedly, but Aussie gave them a hand motion to turn it down a notch. When they settled, he began to speak again.

"A warning to those of you who are thinking you'll get the coordinates and power right through to the end of this challenge. That won't happen. At best, you'll complete the task in four days, and that's with a bit of luck on your side. Most of you have never been to Australia, so I'll tell you what you're getting into. Out here in the Outback, you'll be dealing with critters that you've never seen before, and an unforgiving environment. You've never been in a dark as dark as it gets out here at night. And here's a warning. You'll discover driving out here at night is dangerous. You'll never know when you'll turn a corner too fast and run right into a troop of kangaroos or a herd of cattle. Dehydration could also be an issue, so you need to make sure you've always got enough water, especially when going into longer hikes."

One of the English men raised his hand.

"Yeah, Jim?" Aussie said.

"Jamie," the man corrected. "Will there be a support team in case something bad does happen?"

"Yes, and no," Aussie answered. "In the true spirit of geocaching, if you make poor decisions, you'll have to deal with them. If there is something you can't get out of, or get an injury that needs medical attention, one of our team will help you out. The penalty for that help is that we will pull you from the game. Everyone understand that?"

Every team nodded or verbally acknowledged they did.

A woman with an athletic build and long, wavy brown hair raised her hand.

"Yeah, Zoe?" Aussie said, calling on the woman.

"Are we going to be given anything to help us out? Like anything we'd normally carry with us while geocaching, or any supplies?"

"You'll get two things. One is a rental car. The other is a credit card you can use for petrol and any other needs as you see fit."

As if on cue, Jake moved from table to table, passing out the credit cards to each of the team leaders. When he finished, he moved to Aussie and whispered something in his ear. Aussie nodded, then turned his attention back to the geocachers.

"Bad news. My mate has told me there was a mix-up with the cars. They'll be here in the morning."

Across the table from Allie, Caleb raised his hand.

"Yeah?"

"Is the first stage of the geocache something we can find on foot if we wanted to not wait for the cars to arrive?"

Aussie smiled. "Like I said, it's up to your own free will to decide what to do. But I'll give you this one for free. That would be the worst decision you could make. Enjoy the day, get a good night's rest, and get a fresh start in the morning. Any other questions?"

No one in the group had one, so as Aussie stepped away from the lectern, Jake did another loop around the tables, passing out envelopes.

When Allie got her envelope, she opened it immediately. Inside was a letter-sized sheet of common white paper, on which was displayed a single set of coordinates. She laid the sheet on the table so her friends could see it.

"That's not much to go on," Drake said. "No description and no hints. No difficulty or terrain rating."

"Are you surprised? Everyone here is supposed to be the cream of the crop when it comes to geocaching," Geneva said. "What did you expect them to do, drive you right up to the cache location and have a bright blinking arrow point right at the container? At least they gave us the starting coordinates."

"That's true. They could have just given us a puzzle and told us to figure out the starting coordinates. Would you have preferred that, Drake?" Allie asked.

Drake smirked, then shook his head, knowing full well everyone in his group knew of his disdain for mystery caches, where you had to solve some sort of puzzle or riddle to get the actual coordinates to the geocache. "Doesn't matter to me. Allie's the one in charge of figuring those out."

"Since the car's not available until tomorrow, what should we do with the rest of the day?" Allie asked.

"We could see what we have for resources," Ingrid said. "And maybe see if there is a shop nearby where we could stock up on water and protein bars and stuff like that."

"Good idea," Allie said.

"We should also check out those coordinates and see where they lead," Geneva said. "Finding a map of the area wouldn't hurt."

Allie nodded. "Drake?"

Allie watched him for a few seconds when he didn't answer her. He looked busy bunching up the tablecloth and then smoothing it flat again. When he'd repeated the action twice more, Allie put her hand on his forearm.

"Drake? Are you doing okay, buddy?"

Drake looked Allie in the eye. They were the same old hazel eyes he always had, but some of the sparkle seemed to have gone missing.

"Yeah," he said after an awkward pause. "I'm good. Still tired from the flight down. Would you be okay if I went for a nap? Give me fifteen minutes and then I'll be up for whatever you want."

Geneva, Ingrid, and Allie stared at Drake as he rose from the table, pushed in his chair, and left the room. He moved with a tentative shuffle, with shoulders slouched, like he'd aged fifty years over the last hour.

"What's going on with him?" Geneva asked.

"I'm not sure," Allie said. "Hopefully it is just sleepiness. Keep an eye on him, though. Just in case there's something else going on that we need to worry about. First things first. Everyone go get anything related to geocaching, and let's meet back here in ten minutes."

The women agreed, then left the conference room. Allie and Ingrid walked together to their room, and when they opened the door, they found their carry-on bags and backpacks lined up neatly in the bathroom shower stall.

"What's this about?" Ingrid asked as she retrieved her bags and carried them into the main room. She set her carry-on bag on the floor next to the desk, and her backpack on the desk. She opened it and started pulling from it anything that would help her on a geocaching quest.

"That's Drake," Allie answered. "He's a little paranoid about bedbugs, so he always puts his luggage in the tub until he can check the bedding and everywhere else for the critters."

"Oh," Ingrid said. "Is that something we should do?"

Allie checked the bed and noticed someone had pulled the covers back, then hastily replaced them. "I'm certain he's already done it for us. Back in a minute."

Allie went to the bathroom, used the facilities, washed her hands, and returned with her luggage. She set her carry-on bag on the bed. She opened her backpack and unceremoniously dumped everything from it onto the comforter. From it, she made two piles. Things usable while on the hunt, and things she could leave behind. When she finished, she placed all the things she needed into the pack and closed it.

"You ready?" Allie asked.

Ingrid nodded, and they made their way back to the conference room, where they found Geneva already waiting for them.

"How's Drake?" Allie asked.

"Sleeping like a baby. He woke long enough to show me where his stuff was, then fell back asleep right away," Geneva answered.

Allie nodded, then opened her backpack and dropped all the contents onto the table and organized them into a tidy display. Ingrid and Geneva followed suit, and soon there was a pile of items in front of them.

"Let's see," Allie said as she took stock of the haul. "We've got three tweezers, three hand mirrors, a magnet, a dental mirror, four notebooks, a small first aid kit, a multi-tool, a dozen pens, a mini-flashlight, paperclips, extra batteries, two handheld GPSs and one for the car. And four backpacks to carry everything in. What are we missing?"

The women stared at the pile for a minute.

"The only other thing I would normally take out with me is my hiking stick, and I couldn't get on the plane with that," Geneva said. "Otherwise, I'd say we have a good stock of the basics."

"So, I guess it's down to getting some supplies and a map," Allie said.

"I talked to the girl at the front desk," Geneva said. "There's a grocery store two blocks from here, and she has a basic city map, along with a regional one at the desk we can have."

"Good, then we just need a few supplies. Let's go shopping."

CHAPTER FOUR

Allie woke to a gentle rapping on her hotel room door. She looked at the digital clock on the nightstand, saw it was seven o'clock on the dot, and got out of bed.

"Yeah?" she said through the closed door.

"Ms. Ashe, I've got your car keys," a male voice said.

"Hold on." Allie left the door and picked a sweatshirt off of the chair. It was Ingrid's, but it fit Allie fine. She put the sweatshirt on, then inhaled deeply, breathing in Ingrid's scent. Somewhat dressed, Allie stepped back to the door and opened it with the security chain still on.

"Morning," Zeke said. "I've got the keys to your Jeep Wrangler. It's all gassed up and in the hotel parking lot out back. Your Jeep is the only yellow one back there."

"Thanks," Allie said.

Zeke passed the key through the barely open door and smiled at her. "You have a fun and safe day now."

Allie nodded and closed the door.

"Who was that?" Ingrid asked. She sat up in bed, yawned, and stretched her arms over her head.

"Zeke, dropping off the car keys." Allie held them up and jingled them.

"What time is it?" Ingrid asked.

"Seven. Too early."

"Should we get up and get going?"

Before Allie could answer, there was another knock at the door. Thinking it was Zeke again, she opened the door without looking through the peephole.

"Well, good morning," Geneva said when Allie opened the door.

Allie closed the door, undid the chain, and opened it wide.

"Are you guys ready to go?" Geneva asked, pushing her way into the room with Drake right on her heels.

When Ingrid saw the two enter the room, she slid farther under the covers.

Geneva saw a lump in the bed, the approximate size of her friend, and Allie's tousled hair. "I guess not. Why don't Drake and I go find some breakfast, and we'll meet you in the lobby?"

Geneva spun around and pushed Drake from the room. "See ya," she said without looking back as the door closed behind her.

"That was embarrassing," Ingrid said, throwing off the covers.

Allie shrugged. "I've gotten caught doing worse. Let's get going."

Forty minutes later, Allie and Ingrid stepped into the lobby and found Geneva and Drake sitting in chairs. Geneva was working her way through a magazine. Drake was messing with his phone. When she spotted the women coming toward them, Geneva held up a white paper bag.

"We got you some cronuts," she said.

"Some what?" Ingrid asked.

"A cronut. It's half croissant, half donut. It's delicious. Even Drake had one and liked it."

Ingrid pulled one from the bag and studied the pastry. It was round like a donut, and had a hole like a donut, and had icing on top like a donut, but the texture of the pastry itself had flaky layers like a croissant. She took a bite, decided it was one of the most fabulous things she'd ever eaten, and devoured the rest of it. After watching Ingrid, Allie reached into the bag for a pastry of her own.

When she finished, Allie dug the Jeep keys out of her pocket and held them up. "Who has the map, the coordinates, and the GPS?"

Geneva reached into her bag and pulled out a Garmin Nuvi, along with a car charger. Drake was sitting on the maps, and Allie pulled the coordinate sheet from her pocket. She handed the paper to Geneva, who entered the longitude and latitude into the GPS, and hit the little green button to calculate the route. The machine took a moment to grab its location from a satellite, then displayed the driving route and the time of arrival.

"It's about a twenty-two-minute ride from here," Geneva said. "Not too bad, though, right off a main road."

The group walked to the parking lot of the hotel, and in the second row, they found the yellow Jeep Wrangler standing out like a banana in a bowl of limes.

"Who wants to drive?" Allie asked.

"I will," Drake said as he opened the car door. "Hey, what's this?"

Where he was used to the driver's seat being was the passenger seat. Sitting behind the wheel was Ingrid, beaming at him.

"That's the wrong side of the car," Ingrid said.

"Uh, I meant I wanted to ride shotgun," Drake countered as he climbed into the passenger seat.

"Sure, you did," Ingrid teased. She held out her hand and Allie dropped the car keys into it.

Ingrid started the Jeep and took a moment to familiarize herself with all the controls and knobs. While she did that, Drake fiddled with the radio and found a station playing classic American rock and roll as Geneva and Allie climbed into the back seats and buckled up. Geneva passed the GPS forward, and Drake plugged it in and attached it to the windshield with a suction cup.

"Everyone ready to go?" Ingrid asked. She looked in the rear-view mirror, saw Allie giving a thumb's up, and backed out of the parking space.

The lot had only a few cars in it, so Ingrid did a few circles around the lot to get used to being on the wrong side of the car and then pulled out into traffic. She drove south through town and turned left on a highway, following the pink line on the GPS. She followed the highway straight for ten minutes and then turned off the road and into a wayside. Ingrid navigated the dirt road and pulled the Jeep in between two other cars into the only remaining spot and shut down the engine.

"Where to from here?" Allie asked once they were all standing in the parking lot.

Long, narrow leaves of ghost gum trees that stood around the lot's perimeter shaded the parking lot. Each tree had striking smooth, white bark that appeared ghostly in the morning sun.

Drake and Geneva each had a handheld GPS unit, booted them up, and entered in the coordinates. Drake's unit hit on the coordinates first, and an arrow on the display pointed him in the correct direction.

"It's three-tenths of a mile that way," Drake said, pointing the way of the arrow.

"They use meters down here," Ingrid said.

Drake looked at his Garmin and shrugged. "Not me. I'm set to feet and have no intention of changing it. Let's go."

Drake took off, headed for a clearly marked trailhead, kicking up dust with his boots as he walked. The women, not wanting to be in the cloud of dirt, stayed two yards behind him as they followed. The trail narrowed to four feet wide between two rock outcroppings and, after a few yards, opened up to an expanse of over thirty feet, like the group had simply walked through the wrong end of a funnel and into a gulch.

Beneath their feet, the earth was a mixture of hard-packed dirt and sand, each the color of faded brick, and the walls of rock on either side of them looked forged of earth in red, orange, and brown hues. They started out forty-feet tall on either side, and gently sloped toward ground level the farther they walked. Since the trail widened, the girls caught up to Drake and walked beside him rather than behind him.

Geneva checked her GPS and moved diagonally to the sheer rock wall of the outcropping to her right. She stopped a foot in front of the wall, and Drake appeared at her side a few seconds later.

"I've got fifteen more feet that way," Geneva said. "What do you have?"

"Eighteen," Drake said, checking his display. "I guess we need to go up."

Geneva reached out, put her hand on the wall, and looked up at the almost vertical face before her. "How do you propose we get up there?"

Drake looked up, then at everyone there. "Well," he said, taking off his Titans cap and running his fingers through his hair before replacing it. "We could stand on each other's shoulders."

Allie smirked. "Wouldn't it be easier if we walked to the end of the wall and followed the natural slope back up it?"

Drake flashed her a smile. "Sure. That would be way easier, but not nearly as much fun."

As one, the group turned away from the wall and followed the ridge as, foot by foot, it sloped to their level. At the point where it was but a few inches above the flat earth, Drake stepped up and offered his hand to help his friends take the first step.

Allie took a few steps up the slope. As she wasn't a fan of heights, she hoped the ridge was wide enough to squelch her general anxiety about climbing it without worrying about falling over the edge. She studied the landscape to her right and realized she didn't need to worry, as the ridge went on for at least a few hundred yards before it reached the other side. She moved ten yards away from the edge and started climbing the ridge in earnest. The farther she ascended, the more the landscape opened up to her. She stopped, turned to her right, and looked across the expanse of land beyond. All shaded in the same tones of the ridge on which she currently stood, and all dotted with trees against the backdrop of the largest bright blue sky she'd ever seen.

"Pretty, isn't it?" Geneva asked.

Allie hadn't noticed Geneva's approach until she spoke. "Yes, it sure is." She scanned the horizon for another full minute, then turned and continued her ascent up the slope. Since she'd stopped to take in the view, everyone else had taken a lead on her. Drake was way ahead of the rest of the group and was zeroing in on a tree near the top of the rise, and Ingrid was only a few yards behind him. Geneva, having stopped for a moment with Allie, was halfway between Ingrid and Allie, and since she appeared to be half mountain goat, she was closing the distance fast.

Allie picked up her pace and met the group near the lone ghost gum tree in the area. When she got to Drake's side, he checked the screen and looked at the tree.

"I'm at one foot right here," Drake said.

Geneva checked her machine and wandered a few feet away. "I'm at zero feet here."

Allie looked at where Geneva stood on open ground. "There's nothing over there. It's probably on this tree."

The group started searching the tree trunk for anything that resembled a geocache container. The trunk contained a small hole near the ground, and Drake dropped to his knees, bent over, and peered into the hole. He stuck his hand in, then pulled it out immediately.

"Snake!" Drake screeched. He pushed against the tree hard enough to lose his balance. He did a backward somersault and ended up flat on his back in the dirt.

Ingrid and Geneva, having had an unpleasant experience with rattlesnakes in the Arizona desert, slowly backed away from the tree a few paces. Allie, the ever-curious one, found a stick the length of her forearm on the ground, approached the hole, and crouched. With a quick motion, she thrust her stick in the hole and moved it about like she was mixing up a cake batter, and withdrew the stick. She waited for something to happen, and when nothing did, she repeated the action. Nothing came rushing or slithering out of the hole the second time, either, so Allie dropped to her knees and gazed into the dark void.

"Holy crap, Drake. You stumbled onto something here," Allie said.

"What?" Drake said, having gotten himself into a sitting position.

"The rare and mystifying Australian stick snake."

Allie reached in the gap and from it withdrew a stick that was seven inches long, and two-inches thick. The dried bark was peeling away, making it resemble a snake shedding its skin. She tossed it in Drake's direction. It bounced once, then came to rest against his jeans right between his legs.

"Funny, Allie. Funny." Drake picked up the stick and tossed it away. He got to his feet and brushed the dust from the back of his jeans and made his way back to the tree. "Anything in there?"

"Flashlight," Allie ordered.

Ingrid's was the first one in hand, so Allie took it and shined the light into the hole. "Nope. It's empty."

"It's got to be on this tree somewhere," Geneva said. She did another pass around the tree, feeling for crevices she might have missed.

"Is it up higher?" Ingrid asked.

The lowest branch was ten feet above their heads, and Drake, being the tallest, searched as high on the trunk as he could.

"Maybe it was on Drake's stick snake," Geneva said. "Where did you put it?"

"I tossed it over there," Drake said with a point of his finger.

Geneva moved to the stick, picked it up, and studied it intently.

"Well? Do you see anything?" Ingrid asked.

Geneva turned the stick over in her hand and went so far as to peel away some of the remaining bark. "Nope. Sometimes, apparently, a stick is only a stick."

Geneva dropped the stick and watched it fall to the ground. It hit on one end, then rolled a few inches and came to a stop. She spotted something odd and leaned over for a closer look.

"Hey, guys. Come here," Geneva said. She stood still while her friends gathered around her. "What do you suppose that is?"

The four stood in a rough square and looked at the ground where Geneva was pointing.

On the ground, carved into the top of the ridge, were a group of six concentric circles, starting at a hole in the center and expanding outward, each about an inch away from the previous circle.

"It's a bunch of circles," Drake said. "Someone put circles on the rock."

"Yeah, but why?" Allie asked. "That's a weird thing to do."

Allie removed her cell phone from her pocket and snapped off a couple of quick pictures of the anomaly. Next, she zoomed in for another photo.

"Hey. There's something in there," Allie said.

"Where?" Drake asked, bending over. "There's nothing but circles."

Allie looked up at Drake, spotted the pen he had tucked between his right ear and his hat, and snatched it from him. The pen was a ballpoint, so she took the hard plastic cap from the pen, inverted it, and used the clip end to pop a small metal washer from the hole. She took the washer between her fingers and handed Drake his pen.

"How in the world did you spot that?" Drake asked.

"It caught the sun's reflection when I took the photo."

Tied to the washer was a length of near-transparent fishing line that fed into the hole. Allie pulled on the line, felt some tension, and started pulling up the line. As Allie pulled, the line coiled randomly around the hole. After three feet, a small plastic vial attached to the line appeared. Allie kept tugging, and after another foot, another vial appeared. She pulled up another two feet of line and got to the end when she extracted a heavy lead weight.

Allie grabbed the first vial and gently unscrewed the top. She inverted the vial and tapped it on her hand and a small piece of paper rolled like a scroll fell into her palm. She unrolled the paper and on it spotted a set of coordinates. With her phone, she snapped a picture, then rolled the paper back up and returned it to the vial. Then she repeated the process with the second vial. On the paper there, she discovered a list of four symbols. She took another picture and placed the paper back in the vial and sealed it up. Careful not to knot the line, she put the lead piece into the hole and slowly fed the line in until the vials were both in the hole and she had only the washer between her fingers. She placed that in the hole, then carefully maneuvered it so it sat the way it was when she found it.

"What did you find?" Drake asked.

"Hush," Geneva interrupted. "Does anyone hear voices?"

The group fell silent, and sure enough, off in the distance, they heard someone calling out for someone to wait a moment.

Allie waved her hands forward, and her friends took the hint and walked with her away from the spot. When they had almost got back to the tree, they spotted a woman with wavy blond hair and a bright, friendly face coming into view. The woman waved, then picked up the pace and stopped right next to Geneva.

"Whew, that was quite the hike up, wasn't it?" she said in a bright English accent. "We didn't get introduced yesterday. My name is Sophie Parker. That stocky fellow with the sandy blond hair is my husband. We're from London, as are the Thompsons. That's Will and Liz. We're on the same team, you know. Who are you?"

"I'm Geneva. Ingrid, Allie, and Drake," Geneva said, pointing at each person as she named them.

"Bloody good view up here, isn't it? Have you ever seen such a place? Have you ever been here before? We never have. We've geocached all over Europe, of course, and some in the states, but never down here." Sophie stopped speaking, more so because she ran out of breath than for any other reason.

"Sophie, are you badgering these poor people?" Jamie asked when he finally caught up to his wife.

"Of course not. We're simply getting to know each other. This is Genevieve, Iris, Alison, and Dave. They're from… I'm sorry, I didn't catch that. Where did you say you were from?"

"We didn't," Geneva said. Geneva held out her hand. "I'm Geneva. That's Ingrid, Allie, and Drake. Ingrid and I are from Boston. Drake and Allie are from Nashville."

"Boston?" Sophie said. "That's where they had that bell thing, right? Jamie, you remember going there, don't you?"

"No dear, that was Philadelphia. I'm so sorry. She's not good with names or places. But she can find geocaches like a bloodhound, can't you, dear?"

Sophie smiled.

"Ah, let me introduce you to the Thompsons," Jamie said, just as they arrived.

Jamie made the introductions, and everyone shook hands with everyone else.

"Have you found this cache?" Will asked.

Drake nodded. "Just where you'd expect it to be."

"I assume since this is a multi-cache, all that's there are the coordinates to the next stage?"

"Yep," Drake said.

"I don't suppose, in the interests of international relations, you'll just give us the coordinates?" Will said.

"William!" Liz scolded as she playfully smacked her husband on the shoulder. "I apologize. He's kidding."

Will shrugged. "Didn't hurt to ask. Tell us this. Have you seen any other teams here?"

Allie shook her head. "We have not. There was no one else when we got here, and you're the first team we've seen since yesterday."

The two groups stood in awkward silence for a minute.

"I suppose we'd better get at it then," Jamie said.

Allie nodded. "See you on the trail."

CHAPTER FIVE

When they returned to the Jeep, Drake put the new coordinates into the Garmin and waited while it brought up the route.

Ingrid got her bearings, confirmed the route, and drove back to the main road. Once there, she turned right, headed toward Alice Springs. When they got close to town, she caught a highway going south, which led deeper into the Outback. Ingrid pushed the accelerator to the floor, and they took off down the highway.

Drake eyed the speedometer. "Aren't you going a little fast?"

Ingrid shrugged. "What are the odds there's going to be a cop out here?"

Off in the distance, Drake spotted a car headed in their direction. Because of the space between them, he couldn't determine the make or model and could only tell it was a white sedan of some sort. When Ingrid pressed the accelerator a little harder, Drake opened his window an inch, then nonchalantly seized the grab handle above his door. There was a bit of debris in the road that looked like a piece of tire. Drake wondered if Ingrid would swerve to avoid it, but she caught it with the rear tire of the Jeep. Drake watched as the rubber flew into the air, then bounced along the ground until it finally came to rest off the highway.

"Ingrid. Maybe you are going a little too fast."

"Drake. I said not to worry. I'm in complete control of this Jeep, and I've got a need for speed."

Drake looked up and saw the car approaching them was nearby. As it passed, Drake noticed the red and blue lights on the top. Ingrid must have noticed them finally, too, as the engine quieted as she took her foot off of the accelerator. Drake thought they were in the clear, but once the Kia Stinger got past them, it did a quick U-turn and turned on the light bar.

"Oh, bugger", Ingrid said as she tapped on the brakes and turned her directional signal on to show she intended to pull over. She slowed and moved onto the side of the highway, parked, rolled down her window, turned off the engine, and melted into her seat, waiting for the long arm of the law.

Ingrid glanced out of her side mirror and waited. A minute later, a police officer got out of their car, checked for traffic, and approached the Jeep.

"G'day," the officer said. "I'm Officer Martin with the Northern Territory Police. Do you know why I pulled you over?"

Ingrid smiled. Officer Martin was a tall blond, and when she took off her sunglasses, Ingrid noticed she had a lovely pair of green eyes, and, of course, a captivating Australian accent.

"No," Ingrid said.

"Let me give you a hint. The speed limit on this highway is one-thirty kilometers per hour. Would you like to guess how fast you were going?"

Ingrid shrugged. "One-forty?"

"You're close. One-fifty-two. Which is much too fast. Can I have your license?"

"It's in the back. Can I get out?" Ingrid said.

"Certainly," Officer Martin said as she stepped aside. "Mind the traffic."

Ingrid checked her side mirror, saw the road looked clear, and opened the door. She moved to the rear, opened the back door, and fished through her backpack for her wallet. She dug out her driver's license and passed it to the officer.

"American, huh?"

Without waiting, Officer Martin returned to her car while Ingrid remained by the Jeep's rear. An eternity passed as Ingrid stayed put, and the more time passed, the more anxious she became about receiving a ticket, or going to jail, or being deported from the country. At long last, the cruiser door opened, and Officer Martin walked toward Ingrid.

"I could arrest you for reckless driving, but I'm going to cut you a break and give you a written warning instead."

Ingrid smiled. "Thank you."

"Sign here on this line. It's not an admission of guilt, just that you acknowledge you and I had this little talk."

Officer Martin handed Ingrid a pen, and Ingrid affixed her signature to the form. Officer Martin tore off a copy for Ingrid, who folded it in half and tucked it into her pocket.

"Thanks again, I appreciate it," Ingrid said.

"If you want to thank me, watch your speed. If there's one thing I hate about my job, it's scraping tourists off the pavement." The officer retreated to her vehicle while Ingrid shoved her license and her warning into her backpack, closed the Jeep and climbed back behind the wheel.

"Well? What happened?" Drake asked.

"She let me off with a warning," Ingrid said as her cheeks flushed pink with embarrassment.

"How fast were you going?" Geneva asked from the back seat.

"She said she clocked me doing one-fifty-two in a one-thirty," Ingrid admitted.

Geneva was silent for a moment while she calculated the conversions. "Ingrid! That's like ninety-four in an eighty. You're lucky you got off with a warning."

"Yeah, I know," Ingrid said. She started the Jeep, checked for oncoming cars, and pulled back onto the road.

Drake exhaled, released his hand from the grab bar, and rested his forearm on the door frame.

While Ingrid concentrated on staying within a needle's width of the speed limit, Drake dozed, and Allie and Geneva made small talk over the course of an hour. The GPS ordered Ingrid to turn right off the highway, and she did. Although there was a faded street sign attached to an ancient iron post, the road she turned onto had pavement for only a hundred yards before it turned to hard-packed earth.

"This can't be it, can it?" Geneva asked as she looked at the road ahead, showing nothing but the promise of more dirt for miles around.

The Jeep lurched as Ingrid hit a pothole, causing Drake and Allie to bounce in their seats.

"Sorry," Ingrid said. She moved more to the center of the road to avoid a series of upcoming ruts.

"Could you slow down a little?" Drake asked.

Ingrid checked the speedometer, then realized she hadn't seen a speed limit sign since they'd left the highway. Regardless, she dropped her speed by about a quarter, and Drake released his grip on the grab bar. They traveled for another three miles, and the GPS advised Ingrid to turn left on Miner's Road. She kept an eye on the GPS, watching as the distance to turn number ticked down, and when it got below four hundred feet, she slowed to a crawl. Ingrid spotted the corner, then stopped.

"Is that the road?" Ingrid asked, staring at the entrance.

The road looked wide enough to support heavy machinery, but four concrete barriers restricted their way. At some point, the path had been closed completely, but someone had pulled one barrier away and made room for a vehicle to pass through.

"Looks like someone has already been here," Ingrid said.

"There are fresh tracks in the dirt."

"There's a couple of them," Drake said. "Perhaps there's someone already here." He waved his hand in a manner that Ingrid should get going.

Slowly, so as not hit the barriers on either side, Ingrid passed through and crept down the non-maintained road. They drove for about a mile when they crested a hill and spotted the remains of a mining town in a valley below them. The town, so much as it was, held only one standing building, and the skeletons of four more. All the wooden structures were bleached gray from the sun, except the charred remains of one that burned almost completely away, its vertical support beams standing erect and giving the only indication of how large the building had originally been. A mine entrance stood on the far side of buildings. It cut into the side of a ridge opposite from where they were.

"Miner's Road led to a mine. Go figure," Drake said.
Ingrid ignored the remark and followed the tire tracks on the road as it descended into the valley. When she got to the valley floor, she noticed the single set of tire tracks broke into three. One stopped nearby, one headed toward the only remaining building, and one continued on to the mine itself. Rather than follow all the tracks, she let the Garmin take her where the coordinates marked ground zero, which was by the building.

"Okay, everyone out," Ingrid said as she parked the car and turned off the engine. "Where are we going? Into the building?" Geneva checked her Garmin and gestured to the structure. "In there."

The four geocachers made their way to the building and stepped through the entry, which was missing a door. Also missing was glass from every window, and all the roofing on one half of the building, allowing the sun to stream inside. The structure, ten feet square, contained a yellow metal desk, and behind the desk was a chair with no seat. Every wall contained graffiti, including a full-blown mural featuring Uluru that took up the entire north wall. Amazingly, no one dared to put so much as a stray pencil mark on the mural.

"Well, where should we look?" Drake asked. "Desk is the obvious location. I don't relish trying to find coordinates on those walls."

Drake moved the chair away from the desk and started pulling out drawers. The middle drawer came out easily, and inside Drake spotted someone's rock collection, which filled the entire drawer. He picked one up at random, studied it for any potential clues, and put it back. He repeated the process with several rocks, but, finding nothing, he placed them all back in the drawer and closed it.

To his left and right were two drawers on each side. He started with the top drawer on his left. It opened with a screech of metal upon metal, and Drake peered in, finding nothing. He slammed the drawer and opened the bottom one.

"Well, here's something interesting," Drake said.

From the drawer, he pulled a turtle shell and placed it on the desk in front of him.

"Cool," Geneva said. She moved forward, picked up the shell, and examined it for coordinates or clues. "Nope. Nothing we need, but some poor turtle is running around without pajamas."

Ingrid laughed, Allie rolled her eyes, and Drake made no response at all as he returned the shell to the drawer. When he opened the bottom drawer, he discovered a stack of newspapers and dropped them on the desk.

Drake moaned. "If it comes to reading through these or scouring the walls for coordinates, I'd rather start with the walls."

Allie stepped forward and picked the top paper from the stack. "June 1984. Good year, I hear."

"Was it?" Geneva asked.

Allie shrugged. "Couldn't really tell you. Ask my parents.

Drake's right. It would take us hours to find anything in these papers." Allie dropped it back on the stack. "What else you got in there?"

Drake turned his attention to the top drawer to his right and yanked. It didn't budge. He stepped closer, put both hands on the handle, and pulled, grunting as he did so, as if the guttural sound would add more strength. When it didn't open again, he pulled a third time. With the groan of ripping metal, the handle separated from the drawer. Drake stepped back, tripped over the discarded chair, pinwheeled his arms to try to regain his balance, then finally fell onto the floor.

Geneva rushed to his side. "Drake? Are you okay?"

Drake moaned, then rolled over, clutching at his back. "I think I landed on something."

"Let me look," Geneva said.

She leaned down and picked a rock out from under Drake's back. "Just a little stone. Barely the size of a pea."

Drake sat up and took the stone from Geneva's fingers. He looked at it, then tossed it over his shoulder. Although Geneva seemed genuinely concerned for him, Allie and Ingrid were doing their best to suppress laughter.

"What's so funny?" Drake asked.

Allie smiled, then swallowed hard. "Oh, nothing. Just this." Allie did an exaggerated impression of Drake flailing his arms, then stepped backward, and in slow-motion dropped to her knees and onto her back. She started giggling, which prompted Ingrid to break out in laughter as well.

"Not funny, Allie," Drake protested. He looked up at Geneva, and although she wasn't laughing, she had a smile spread from ear to ear. "Help me up, will you?"

Drake held out his hand, and Geneva got him to his feet. Once vertical, he dusted off his pants and moved to the last drawer.

"I hope there's something good in this one," Allie said,

joining him back at the desk.

"Let's find out."

Drake pulled on the handle, and again, it didn't budge. He emitted a long sigh, braced himself, and pulled again. This time, with a screech of metal, the drawer came loose and fell free from the desk, landing on the floor three feet away from the desk with a clang, like someone had kicked a metal trashcan. Drake moved to the drawer, bent over, took a quick look, then backed away in haste, tripping over the chair a second time. He landed on his rear and immediately pointed toward the drawer. "Snake!"

"Funny, Drake," Allie said.

Drake got back to his feet and pointed again at the drawer. "Seriously. There's a snake in there."

Allie rolled her eyes, then moved around the desk and toward the drawer. She stopped on a dime when a triangular dark olive head with bands of yellow appeared over the side. Allie stepped back slowly until she moved right into Geneva.

The snake stood still for a moment, except for its tongue that flicked in and out, collecting the scents of the humans in the area. The snake rose higher from the drawer, its dark eyes shining in the sun, then escaped the drawer and slithered its way toward the door.

When the tail disappeared, Allie exhaled. "Did you see that? That snake must have been five feet long."

"I told you," Drake said. "I told you there was a damn snake in there."

Allie moved to the drawer, stopped a couple feet away, leaned over and looked in.

"Is there another snake in there?" Ingrid asked.

Allie picked up the drawer and set it on the desk. "Who's got a light?"

Ingrid passed her flashlight to Allie, who shined it on the side of the drawer. Scratched on the surface were a set of coordinates. Allie read them off and Geneva wrote them down.

"What's that under the coordinates?" Ingrid asked.

"It says L-one to L-four," Allie said, reading the scratches.

"What's that mean?" Drake asked.

"Your guess is as good as mine," Geneva said. "Let's load in the coordinates and see where they lead. Maybe that will give us an idea." Geneva placed the new waypoints into her machine and waited for the arrow to guide the way. "The new coords are taking us four hundred feet in that direction," she said, pointing to the north.

"So, we need to go into the mine?" Ingrid asked.

"Isn't it that way?" Drake asked, pointing to the west.

"No. I think it was north. Let's go outside and see," Geneva said.

Geneva led the group outside, and they walked around the building. Geneva's arrow pointed directly at the mine's entrance.

"I'm not so sure about this," Allie said. "You know how I feel about underground caches."

Drake shook his head. "I never understood how you could serve in active combat in the Marines but have trouble going through a tunnel."

Allie stopped and put her hands on her hips in indignation. "Because, Duck-man, you've never been in a crumbling foxhole treating someone with internal bleeding and missing half of a leg. With the walls caving in, it's like you're being buried alive with the person you are trying to save."

Drake stayed silent for a moment, not knowing what to say. "Point taken."

Ingrid took Allie by the arm. "Come on. Let's at least see how far into the mine the coordinates take us." Ingrid pulled Allie's arm, but Allie stayed planted where she stood. "Let's go, Allie. You can do this." Ingrid yanked again, and this time, Allie allowed herself to be moved toward the mine.

When they got to the shaft, they stopped to take it all in visually. Before the entrance there was a sturdy-looking tunnel built from wood pillars eighteen-inches square. The roof appeared built of the same timbers, and although the sun had bleached them gray, they seemed just as steadfast as when workers installed them.

Drake put his hand on the support nearest him and pushed. It didn't budge, bow, or shed a single flake of dust. "Seems fine to me."

"What about that?" Ingrid asked, pointing to a sign lying in the dirt a few feet from the entrance. On it, someone had hand-painted, now-faded red lettering that said not to enter the abandoned mine.

Geneva checked the display of her GPS. "It says we need to go another fifty feet in, so I guess we ignore the sign? I'm assuming everything we encounter here will be safe."

"Who's got the flashlight?" Drake asked.

Allie took it from her pocket and handed it to him. He clicked it on, and headed for the entrance, Geneva right behind him.

"Are you good to do this?" Ingrid asked.

Allie hesitated, then nodded. "Sure. Why not? What's the worst that can happen in an abandoned mine we're not supposed to be in?"

Ingrid smiled, took Allie's hand, and led her into the darkness.

CHAPTER SIX

Drake held the only flashlight, but since it was a miniature one, it didn't cast a wide enough beam to pick up everything in the mine entrance. To get more light, Allie, Geneva, and Ingrid activated the flashlight modes on their cell phones, and the immediate area became awash in light.

Once inside the entrance, the walls became bedrock, shored up by timber every few feet. There were large rocks galore scattered around, mostly near the walls. There were the remnants of an old barrel, a shovel head, and a wood chair. Like the building, most of the walls contained graffiti. A few yards ahead of them, they spotted a steel cage. When they approached, they determined it was an elevator. Farther on, a tunnel sloped down into the mine.

"What does your GPS say, Geneva?" Drake asked.

Geneva trained her flashlight on the screen. "It says no satellite reception. I think we're on our own in here."

"You said before we needed to go about fifty feet into the mine. I think we're about there now. Everyone look around," Drake said.

The group fanned out and checked the area for a new set of coordinates. Drake and Ingrid turned over the larger rocks to check if their event hosts had hidden anything underneath. Geneva turned her attention to the graffiti, starting near the door and working her way into the mine. Allie, not wanting to stray too far, hung out by the elevator shaft, her hand on the cage, hoping the lights didn't suddenly go out. Attached to the cage was a wood sign with vinyl letter stickers that designated the current level as level one.

"Hey, guys, come here," Allie said.

"What? Did you find something?" Drake asked, the first to join her.

Allie pointed at the sign. "This looks fairly new, don't you think?"

"Yeah, I guess it does."

"Level one. L one," Allie said. "Hey, you don't suppose..." Rings on each of the signs' top corners connected it to the cage. She lifted the sign. On the other side, vinyl numbers displayed five digits. "It looks like the degrees and minutes of a coordinate."

"Based on this, I guess we need to visit three more levels," Geneva said.

"Looks like it," Allie answered.

Drake moved to the elevator, opened the cage, and shined the flashlight into the shaft. The light illuminated the walls for a few feet, then darkness engulfed it. He stepped back, found the elevator call button, pushed it, and when nothing happened, pushed it again.

"I'm only guessing," Geneva teased, "but I don't think that's going to work."

Drake turned around. "Wishful thinking. Looks like we'll have to walk down. Let's get this over with." Without waiting, Drake pointed the flashlight at the tunnel ahead. "You coming?"

Geneva had to jog to catch up with Drake, but after a few

feet, she did.

"Hey, wait up, you two!" Ingrid yelled, her voice echoing off the walls. Although Ingrid could no longer see Drake and Geneva, she spotted their lights, which had stopped the second she called out. Although the beams floated a bit, reminiscent of fireflies, they no longer moved farther away.

"You don't have to do this if you don't want to," Ingrid said, turning to face Allie.

Allie had a grip on the elevator cage, so Ingrid worked Allie's fingers away from the steel and took both of Allie's hands in hers.

"Seriously. There are three of us down there. You've already shown us what we need to look for. Why don't you sit this one out? It won't take us more than twenty or thirty minutes to get what we need. Why don't you stay here, or step outside?"

"What if you need me?" Allie asked.

Ingrid held up her phone. "I'll call you."

"You think your signal will work underground?"

Ingrid grinned. "Not a chance."

Allie smiled and laughed. "Okay. You've convinced me. I think I'll step outside and wait in the sunshine."
"I'll walk you out."

Ingrid took Allie's hand and led her to the entrance. Once Allie was in the sunlight, Ingrid grinned and kissed Allie on the forehead. "Wait for me. I'll be right back."

Ingrid watched as Allie found a boulder to sit on, then moved back into the tunnel, following the lights that waited for her.

"Is she going to be okay?" Drake asked once Ingrid joined them.

"Yeah. She'll be fine as long as she's out there. Let's get this over with. I'm sure she's worried about us."

So not to trip over anything, the three focused their lights on the floor and began their descent into the dark mine in earnest.

Out in the open, Allie sat on the boulder. After five minutes, the rock beneath her became uncomfortable. After another ten minutes, the sun shifted in the sky, removing a small sliver of shade she had and exposing her to the harsh rays of the Outback. Since she knew she hadn't taken a second to apply any form of sunscreen, she trekked back to the building, stepped inside, and made herself comfortable as best as she could on top of the desk.

A few minutes later, she heard an approaching vehicle, and picked up the sound as car doors opened, and, after a brief hesitation, closed. Allie expected the talkative English woman to come strolling through the door, but it surprised her when two other couples came through the door. One man sported a white hat with a red maple leaf on the front, so Allie surmised the Canadians had caught up with them.

"Hi!" Allie said enthusiastically.

"Hello," one woman said warily.

"Don't worry. I'm a geocacher, too. I'm Allie. From America."

The woman's countenance shifted from one of caution to one of acceptance. "I'm Emily. Claire, Ryan, Daniel," she said, pointing out each person in turn. "Where's the rest of your team?"

Allie liked Emily right off. She was petite and athletic, with shoulder-length auburn hair and bright blue eyes. She had a green, wide-brimmed hat that shaded most of her face, and looked comfortable in her outdoor gear and hiking boots.

Rather than tell her directly, Allie shrugged. "They headed out on a walkabout or something. I came in here to get out of the sun."

"Did you find the coordinates?" Daniel asked. Daniel had an athletic build. He wore no hat to protect him from the sun, so Allie noticed his short black hair that matched his neatly trimmed beard. Like Emily, he wore hiking boots.

"We did."

"Care to give us a hint?" Emily asked.

Allie smiled, then answered. "Yes. Somewhere in this room. Oh, let me get out of your way so you can get to it."

Allie slid down from the desk, smiled at the woman and man she hadn't spoken to, and walked out into the sun. She walked to the shady side of the building, checked the surroundings for snakes and other critters, then sat on the ground, her back to the building and closed her eyes. Behind her, she heard muffled voices, which she ignored. An unknown number of minutes later, she heard footsteps shuffling through the dirt.

"Your friends headed into the mine?"

Allie opened her eyes and noticed Emily standing before her, hands on hips.

"They did," Allie said. She checked the time on her phone. "About twenty-five minutes ago. They should be back any minute now."

"You didn't go with them?"

Allie shook her head. "I've got this thing about going underground."

Emily nodded and turned.

"Good luck," Allie said.

Allie watched Emily walk away and rejoin her group and closed her eyes again. Although the weather was warm in the building's shade, it wasn't unbearable. All she needed to be happy in the moment was a glass of lemonade and a book. Her phone buzzed in her hand, so Allie opened her eyes and refreshed the screen. On it, she spotted a message from a friend back home. She answered the text, then checked the time on her phone. Her friends had been gone for thirty-five minutes.

Concerned, Allie found her feet and wandered to the mine entrance. She turned on her phone and walked into the darkness. She stepped to the elevator cage and stopped.

"Hello?" she called in the dark. Her own voice echoed back at her. "Hello!" she yelled. She waited as her word dissipated and waited for someone, anyone, to answer her. No one did in either an American or Canadian accent.

"Hey!" she called again. Nervous, she began tapping her foot. "Hey!" she yelled into the void, this time drawing out the word for a good ten seconds before she stopped.

This time, there was an answer, a quick shout that rose from the depths of the mine, but she couldn't make out if it came from a male or female, or if it was from one of her friends or not. The voice cut off, and in its place came a fierce rumble. Suddenly, the earth shook beneath her feet, then a cloud of dust appeared from the elevator shaft, causing Allie to shield her eyes with her arm, and back away toward the entrance. The dust plume followed her, and Allie had no choice but to run out into the sunshine and away from the mine's mouth. As she watched, the dust settled upon the earth, and all was quiet again.

Allie ran back into the mine and stopped at the shaft.

"Hello?" she screamed into the void.

"Help!" came a barely audible cry from the tunnel.

"Who's there?" Allie asked.

"Help," the voice said again.

"Damn," Allie said under her breath. She switched on the flashlight function and took a few hesitant steps down the tunnel. She stopped to catch her breath.

"Hello?"

"Help." The voice was closer, but weaker.

Allie steeled herself from her fear, and began power-walking down the tunnel, moving her phone's light back and forth, trying to spot the source of the voice. She'd walked twenty yards when she kicked something soft, staggered forward, almost fell, but regained her balance. She shined the light where she'd tripped and discovered a man lying in a fetal position on the ground.

"Drake?" Allie asked, rushing over to the man. She got him turned over and noticed it was the Canadian she hadn't spoken to. His hat was gone, his head wet with blood.

"Hey, you. Can you hear me?" Allie asked.

The man moaned. "Yeah."

"What's your name?"

"Ryan."

"What happened, Ryan?"

She waited for an answer, didn't get one, and repeated the question.

"Don't know. Some sort of booby trap. The whole tunnel collapsed on level four."

"Is anyone else hurt?"

"I… I don't know. I was on my way back when it happened."

"All right. I'm going to get you up and out of here, okay?" Allie said.

Without waiting for an answer, Allie got Ryan to his feet and half-carried, half-dragged him from the mine. Once outside, she laid him on the ground and assessed his injuries. He had a scalp laceration that needed immediate attention, and a wrist that hung askew.

Allie reached for her backpack and realized it was still in the Jeep. She left Ryan's side, rushed to the Jeep, hoping it was unlocked, and breathed a sigh of relief when the rear door opened. She grabbed her backpack, pawed through it, and realized the first aid kit they carried was with Geneva, and her pack was absent from the car.

"Damn," Allie said, slamming the door.

She turned around, saw the Canadians' Range Rover a few yards away, and ran to that. Their vehicle, too, was unlocked, and she scoured the car for anything that might be useful. The Canadians had stocked up well on provisions, so Allie grabbed a handful of practical items and rushed back to Ryan.

"Hey, Ryan, I'm going to do a little first aid on you, okay?"

Allie started by opening a bottle of water and drizzling it on Ryan's head, washing dirt and silt away from his wound. She stopped for a moment, checked it, and saw it was at least four inches long. In the field she would have stitched it up, but since she lacked the supplies, she folded up a T-shirt, applied it to Ryan's wound and wrapped duct tape around Ryan's head to secure it in place.

Ryan's eyes opened wide, and he reached up with his good arm and grabbed Allie's wrist. "Radio. There's a radio in the glove box. You can call for help." Ryan's grip slackened, and he shut his eyes.

Allie ran to the Range Rover, opened the glove box, and extracted a two-way radio from it.

"Hello? Hello? This is an emergency."

"This is Aussie. What's the problem?"

Allie gave him the situation and their location, and once Aussie confirmed help was on the way, Allie dropped the radio on the seat. She was about to leave the car when she spotted a flashlight in the well of the passenger door. Allie grabbed the light and returned to Ryan. She found him unconscious, but with strong vitals. Blood was darkening the T-shirt, but not as fast as she'd expected.

Allie turned on the flashlight and ran into the mine, following the tunnel as it descended level after level until a gigantic pile of rocks and debris blocked her path.

"Hey! Drake? Ingrid?" Allie yelled.

"Allie?" came the response.

"Drake. What happened? Is everyone okay?"

"We've got a couple of injuries in here. We're all clustered by the shaft."

"Okay. Sit tight. Help is on the way."

Allie left them and ran back up the tunnel. By the time she reached the first level, her shirt was damp with sweat and she was gasping for air. She moved to the shaft, opened the cage, and peered into the darkness.

"Drake!" she yelled.

"Allie? Where are you?"

"I'm back up top at the elevator shaft. Everything all right down there?"

"No. We've got injuries."

"Help is coming. Hopefully, you'll be out of there within the hour."

"I'm not sure they can last an hour, Allie. You need to get us out of here now."

"All right. Give me a moment. Let me figure something out."

Allie looked up from the cage and shined her light around the area. In the center of the cage, she saw a cable descending into the shaft. She stood staring at it for a moment, then decided on a course of action.

Allie ran back to her Jeep and made a silent prayer as she opened up the driver's door. She grinned when she saw the keys in the cup holder. She started the Jeep and drove as far into the mine as she could, which was through the wood entryway, and Allie stopped just as the Jeep's nose entered the mine.

Satisfied with the position of her car, Allie got out, unhooked the winch cable attached to the front, and rolled it out until it all came out of the winch. Allie picked up the hook and carried it into the mine and dropped it by the elevator shaft. She didn't have near-enough light, and since she couldn't hold her phone and execute her plan, she propped her phone on one of the cage's cross braces and adjusted the beam so that as much as the center cable got illuminated as possible.

Allie picked up the hook and moved to the edge of the shaft. She attempted to swing it around the elevator cable, but it hit the side of the cage and fell into the shaft. Allie stopped the fall by stomping on the winch cable, then reeled it back in. A second attempt produced the same result.

She stopped for a moment and carefully assessed her situation. Allie draped the hook over her shoulder, then stepped to the cage. She grabbed a hold of the inside of the cage and stepped off of the ground and into the void. Allie clutched the cage with both hands, the steel cutting into her fingers. She struggled to find a foothold, and panicked, until she kicked at the cage with ferocity. Allie, hands already tired, kicked a last time, and the toe of her right shoe lodged in the cage's mesh.

Allie looked down and noticed the mistake she'd made. Below her, the steel mesh made a diamond pattern, and she positioned her left foot sideways so it slid into the center. She pushed up on her legs, relieving some of the pressure on her hands. Allie removed one hand, shook it until she got some feeling back, and then shook out the other. She grabbed the cage, worked out a plan, then slowly moved to her left.

When she got to the corner, she rested for a minute before moving on. Creeping slowly, she climbed across the back wall, then along the last side before she stepped back on to solid ground. Allie emitted a long, loud sigh. She placed the hook on the winch cable, pulled it taut, and slowly took up the slack, hoping that the hook wouldn't shake loose.

Her luck clicked into overdrive, and the hook moved to the elevator cable and held tight. Allie went to the winch and pulled in all the slack. When the cable tightened, she counted to ten, then shut down the winch. When she went back inside the mine, she saw she'd managed to pull the center cable out into the mine entry.

"Drake!" Allie yelled into the shaft. "Do you see the elevator?"

"No," he yelled.

Allie returned to the Jeep and brought in more cable. After another ten counts, she stopped again.

"See anything yet?" she yelled into the shaft.

"It's here," Drake said. "It's about two feet above where we need it, but we can get in."

"How many people can it hold?" Allie asked.

"The injured can't stand, so maybe four."

"Put the injured on the lift and send up your strongest

person with them," Allie ordered. "Tell me when you're ready to go."

Allie crouched, waiting by the shaft. After a couple of minutes, Drake indicated they were ready. Allie returned to the winch and took in the remaining cable. When she saw the elevator hadn't appeared, she got in the Jeep and backed up twenty feet, then returned to the shaft. Drake was in the elevator, along with Emily and Daniel, who were lying at his feet.

"Help me get them outside," Allie said.

Drake did, and soon the Canadians were lying on the ground next to Ryan. While Allie tended to whatever injuries she could, Drake lowered the elevator back down and retrieved the remaining geocachers. Once there were four able-bodies around her, Allie gave directions on how to make her three patients more comfortable, although none were conscious enough to complain.

Allie was doing her best to check Ryan's head wound without disturbing him when Geneva got her attention.

"Hey, Allie, it looks like help is finally here," Geneva said.

Allie looked to her side and saw several vehicles approaching, one of them an ambulance.

"Good," she said to Geneva. "Can you tell me what happened down there?"

Geneva shook her head. "We were just finishing up getting the last part of the coordinates we needed, then suddenly the Canadians showed up. We talked for a few minutes, then the ceiling fell in, and all hell broke loose."

CHAPTER SEVEN

"Tell me you got the coordinates we need after all that," Allie said as the group walked back to the Jeep.

Allie opened the rear door, sat on the tailgate, and pulled a bottle of water from their supplies. She drank half of it without stopping and used the rest to wash blood from her hands.

"It's amazing the way you jumped in like that," Geneva said. Geneva retrieved another bottle of water, found some napkins, and wet them. "Here. Wipe off your face."

Allie took the napkins and ran them over her face and neck. She felt hot and sticky, and the water felt cool and refreshing. "It was nothing, really. Luckily, my training as a medic kicked in. I hope everyone will be okay."

"They've got a fantastic chance of fully recovering, thanks to you," Aussie said as he approached the group. "Can anyone tell me what happened down there?"

Drake stepped forward. "I don't know if we can. We were gathering the last set of numbers when the Canadians came down. We chatted for a bit, and suddenly there was a loud bang and the roof caved in. "

"Good thing none of you got hurt," Aussie said.

"It was only luck. The three of us were by the elevator shaft. They were farther toward the tunnel when it happened. Ingrid pulled the woman closest to us in farther. The others got hit by falling debris before we could do anything to help them."

Aussie nodded. "Claire mentioned you saved her," he said, turning to Ingrid. "She's grateful, and I'm sure she'll want to talk to you later at some point."

"She shouldn't thank me. Allie saved all of us with her quick thinking and superb medical skills."

Allie's cheeks reddened, and she took a sudden interest in glancing at random rocks.

"I'm sorry about your coordinates," Drake said. "I hope this doesn't mess up the other players."

"Don't worry, mate. We've got contingencies for mishaps at every stop." A car honk got Aussie's attention, and he spun and spotted the crews moving off. "I've got to head back to Alice Springs. Good job today, and good luck going forward."

Aussie walked off, leaving the foursome.

"What should we do next? Go back to town?" Geneva asked. "Allie, do you need to take a rest? You look beat and like you could use a long bath."

Allie closed her eyes and concentrated on her breathing. She was on the back end of an adrenaline high, and was coming down hard. She wanted a nap far more than she wanted a bath. Allie counted to ten in her head, and by the time she got to eight, she could sense herself dozing off.

"Allie?" Ingrid said, snapping Allie out of her potential nap.

"Yeah?"

"Want to go back to town?"

Allie opened her eyes and stared into Ingrid's blue eyes. She did. She wanted a hot meal, a cool drink, and a nap. "Where do the next set of coordinates take us? Is it far from here?"

"We don't know," Drake said. "We've been so busy with

everything here, we haven't looked. Should we?"

Allie closed her eyes and nodded. She felt someone sit on the tailgate next to her and assumed it was Ingrid when she put her arm around Allie and moved Allie's head to her shoulder.

"… which puts us… Allie?"

Allie's eyes flew open, not aware she'd fallen asleep. "What? Drake?"

"I said we got the degrees and minutes on one card, and the seconds on a different one, so we didn't know which went with which. We tried one combination, but that put us in the middle of a public swimming pool, which we assumed wasn't correct, so flipping them around puts us at a location about twelve miles from here."

"How much daylight do we have left?" Allie asked.

Drake stepped aside a few paces so he could see the sun, made an assessment, and rejoined the group. "I'd guess about five hours on the low end."

Allie sighed and pushed herself off the tailgate. She stumbled at first, not realizing how tired her legs were. "All right. Let's go for it."

Without another word, Allie moved around the Jeep, climbed into her seat, donned her seatbelt, and put her head back and closed her eyes.

When everyone else was ready, Ingrid fired up the Jeep and waited for Drake to enter the coordinates into the GPS. Once again, she followed the pink line on the display which led from the mine, and eventually back to the main road. She turned north at the junction, headed in the direction of Alice Springs, and drove for only a few miles before the voice in the GPS instructed her to turn off-road to her right.

Ingrid slowed as she got to the turn, checking the rear-view to make sure there was no one behind her. "Is there even a road there?" she asked.

Drake pointed. "Right there. If you consider tire ruts to be a road, that is."

"Okay. I'm going for it." Ingrid checked for oncoming traffic, noticed none, and turned. She passed over a slight rise, not much larger than a speed bump, and followed the ruts in the dirt as she made her way up a rise, then down the other side. She stopped when she came almost to the top of a wash.

"Well, now what?" Ingrid asked.

"Wait here," Drake said. He undid his seatbelt and left the vehicle.

Ingrid watched as Drake moved to the nose of the car and walked straight ahead. After a few feet, he moved straight down a hill and he resembled the path of a setting sun until, after a few strides, his head disappeared from Ingrid's view.

Ingrid checked the rear-view and locked eyes with Geneva. "How's the hero doing back there?"

Geneva glanced at Allie. "She's sleeping like a baby."

Ingrid nodded, took her hands off the steering wheel, and rested them on her thighs. She adjusted the air conditioning and fiddled with the vents while she waited as patiently as was possible for her. After a few more minutes, she saw the top of Drake's head, and like the rising sun, more came into view as he climbed the hill.

Drake entered the Jeep and grabbed his bottle of water from the holder in the center console. He drank half of the water down, capped his bottle, wiped his mouth on his shirt sleeve, and pointed straight ahead.

"All you need to do is follow the tracks. They'll take you over this short rise, then down a hill into an old riverbed. From there, you'll turn left and follow the river."

"How do you know all that?" Ingrid asked.

"We weren't the first ones here today. There's been three other teams here before us. Maybe four."

Ingrid put the Jeep in Drive and tapped the gas only enough to get her to the top of the mound. For a moment, all she could see was the bright blue sky. Then, trusting Drake, she gave the vehicle more gas, and it crested the hill and they were over and on a twenty-foot slide to the bottom of the riverbed. As they got closer to the bottom, Ingrid spotted the tire tracks of the cars that arrived before her, so she turned as soon as the car was horizontal. She checked the GPS, saw the pink line wanted her to go another four-tenths of a mile, and seeing nothing impeding her progress, she goosed the accelerator and picked up speed.

In the distance, the riverbed looked like it was being swallowed by a small mountain, so rather than use the GPS, she headed right for the entrance and parked directly in front of it.

"Crap. Another cave? Allie's not going to be happy," Geneva said.

"Let's not tell her. Let her sleep and we'll slip in, get what we need, and slip out," Drake said. "Or one of you can stay here in the car with her in case she wakes and is wondering where we all went. Or we could write her a note and pin it to her shirt."

"Drake, I can hear you," Allie said without moving or opening her eyes. "Y'all go. I'll wait right here."

"That's settled then," Drake said. "How far do we have to go in?"

"About thirty feet," Geneva said.

"Brights," Allie mumbled.

"What?" Geneva asked.

"Pull the car up as far as you can. Leave it running. Turn on the bright lights. And leave on the air conditioning."

"You heard her," Drake said to Ingrid.

Ingrid moved the car forward as far as she dared and turned on the brights. Immediately, the tunnel flooded with light.

"Good idea, Allie," Drake said.

Allie's reply was nothing more than a grunt.

Ingrid, Geneva, and Drake all got out of the car and headed down the tunnel. Although the interior surfaces looked much like the mine, the tunnel was much smaller than the mine. The ceiling was at most six feet high and eight feet wide. Rather than the perfect shape of a railroad tunnel, the river tunnel was slightly off center, and flared out the closer the opening got to the ground, resembling a cowboy hat with a dent on one side.

Using the car lights, they had no trouble walking in the cave, and within three minutes, they found what they were looking for. On the ground, near the wall, was a small pyramid made of river rocks. Drake lifted the top rock, and underneath it was a plastic box. He opened the box, and inside were several sheets of paper. Drake picked one up and studied it for a moment. He turned the paper over, saw nothing on the other side, then shuffled through the rest of them.

"They seem to be all the same," Drake said.

"Well, Drake, grab one and let's go," Geneva said.

Drake took one, put the rest in the box, and placed it back in the pyramid. He reached for Geneva's hand, then turned to leave. They'd gotten three steps when they realized Ingrid wasn't behind them.

Geneva pivoted and noticed Ingrid seemed focused on the wall opposite the pyramid.

"What is it?" Geneva asked.

Ingrid pointed at the wall. "Look at these symbols."

Geneva turned her attention to the wall. On it were sixteen symbols, spread in four columns of four. "Hey, Drake, can I see that paper?"

Drake moved closer to Geneva and handed over the paper. On the sheet were several symbols, indicating that there was a cipher for them to solve to get the next set of coordinates.

"None of the symbols on the wall are on this sheet," Geneva said.

Drake took the page and looked for himself. "You're right. So what?"

"So what if this sheet is a red herring?"

"What if the wall is?" Drake countered.

"Hey, guys," Ingrid said, getting in between the two of them. "Let's take a picture of the wall, then we'll have them both and can figure out from there which set gives us the coordinates we need."

Allie woke when someone shook her shoulder. She moved her head, groaned when her neck moved as hard as if cast in cement, then locked eyes with Geneva.

"We're back at the hotel," Geneva said with a smile. "Do you need any help out of your seat?"

"Of course not. I'm not infirm, you know," Allie growled. She realized her tone was much harsher than she meant it to be. "Hey, I'm sorry, Geneva. I really need a nap and a shower. Not necessarily in that order, and perhaps at the same time."

Geneva rubbed Allie's knee. "No offense taken. We've all had a hard day."

Allie pulled herself from the Jeep, trudged into the hotel's back door, and was grateful her room was only four doors down. Ingrid beat her to the door, opened it with her keycard, and held the door, allowing Allie to enter first.

Allie kicked off her shoes next to the door so she wouldn't track any dirt into the suite and set her backpack next to them.

"You mind if I take a shower first?" Allie asked.

"Go ahead," Ingrid said as she took off her shoes and placed them next to Allie's. "I want to get a start on this puzzle." Ingrid waved the paper in the air, like someone who had just won the lottery.

"How do we end up always solving the puzzles?" Allie asked.

"Um. Probably because we actually can? If Geneva had to rely on Drake to figure out a puzzle, they'd never find a mystery cache."

Allie laughed, then stripped off her T-shirt and dropped it on top of her shoes. She moved into the bathroom, turned on the shower, then stripped off her remaining clothes while waiting for the water to warm. She stepped in front of the mirror and took a good look.

When she pulled her ponytail from her hair tie and ran her fingers through her red hair, a bit of dust sprinkled down and settled on the sink. She looked in the mirror and saw she had a streak of mud across her left cheek, and a streak of blood on her right cheek, looking like she was ready to take part in some medieval war games. Allie noticed the fog on the mirror, then stepped into the shower.

Allie took her time beneath the cascading water. She shampooed and conditioned her hair twice, and lathered her entire body twice, and stood under the stream for countless minutes. When she noticed her fingertips were looking like prune skin, she turned off the water and stepped onto the bathmat.

The bathroom had a marked difference from before she entered the shower. The pile of dirty clothes was gone, and Ingrid had laid out Allie's hairbrush, toothbrush, and toothpaste on the sink.

Once she toweled off her body, attended to her hair, and brushed her teeth, Allie made her way into the bedroom where she found a fresh change of clothes waiting for her on the bed. Ingrid had slipped out of her dirty clothes and into sweatpants and a T-shirt, and was at the desk, working on the puzzle.

"How's it going?" Allie asked as she slipped into her clean clothes.

"Good. This wasn't a particularly hard cipher to figure out. Even Drake and Geneva would have gotten it, eventually."

Allie raised an eyebrow. "Really?"

Ingrid snickered. "No way. The cipher is easy. It's the picture I'm having trouble with."

"What picture?"

Allie moved over to the desk and looked over Ingrid's shoulder. She pointed to a symbol on the screen. "That one looks like what we found on the top of that ridge."

"I'll tell you what, you take my phone and figure it out while I go shower. Then we'll meet up with the lovebirds for dinner."

Ingrid put her phone on the desk, pushed the chair away, and headed for the bathroom. Allie picked up the phone and studied the images. After doing a few minutes of research on her phone, she grabbed her keycard and headed for the lobby.

"Can I help you?"

"Hi," Allie hesitated while she read the clerk's name tag. "Kimberly."

Kimberly smiled. "Hi."

"Would you have any idea what these symbols mean?"

Kimberly took the phone in hand, studied the picture for a moment, then passed the phone back. She took a business card from a holder in the front of the desk, turned it over, and wrote an address.

"Who you need to see is Uncle Jarli. You'll find him at this address. If you can go soon, I'll ring him up and tell him to wait."

"He's your uncle?" Allie asked.

"No. 'Uncle' is a title of respect reserved for the elders. You should address him as Jarli until he says otherwise."

"What's his last name?"

Kimberly shrugged. "I don't know if he ever had one."

"Thanks. If you wouldn't mind calling him, we can be on our way in just a few minutes."

Allie left the desk and speed-walked to Drake and Geneva's room. She pounded on the door until Drake finally answered. He looked disheveled, his hair was a mess, and he opened the door shirtless.

"Allie? What's going on?" he said, a look of concern on his face.

"We have an appointment with someone. Put your pants on and grab Geneva. The car leaves in five minutes." Allie didn't wait for a response. She continued down the corridor until she came to her room. She pulled the keycard from her pocket, scanned it, found it didn't work and tried it again only to get a red light on the second pass, too.

"Oh, come on!" Allie said as she jammed the card back in her pocket. She knocked on the door without stopping.

"Who's there?" came the response a moment later.

"It's me, Ingrid, open up."

The lock disengaged, and Ingrid opened the door.

"Are you okay?" Ingrid asked, fresh out of the shower and wrapped in a towel.

Allie stopped for a moment and looked at her girlfriend. "You know, you're beautiful when you're wet."

Ingrid smiled, then blushed.

"You need to get dressed, though. We have five minutes."

"What's the big hurry?" Ingrid asked.

"We have to go see a man about your picture."

CHAPTER EIGHT

Ingrid parked the Jeep in front of the nondescript building of the address Kimberly gave Allie. The brick and wood building, once painted a deep green, had faded, and the bricks had lightened under the hot Australian sun. A large picture window was the focal point of the outside, and hand-painted letters across the window announced the name of the place as The Arrernte Historical and Cultural Centre. Over the window and the entry door was a white awning, and in front was a white painted bench, and on that bench sat an aboriginal woman in her mid-twenties wearing denim shorts, a white cotton T-shirt, and tan sandals. She wore her shoulder-length raven-colored hair free, and her light brown eyes scanned the text of the book she held.

"Do you have an appointment with Uncle?" she asked as Allie reached for the door.

Allie cast her glance at the woman. She set a bookmark in place, closed the book, and cocked a thumb at the window behind her. "Are you going to see Uncle? Is he expecting you? Usually, he likes to head home about this time."

"Kimberly called from the hotel. She said he'd meet with

us."

"You're here about the Rainbow Serpent, then?"

"The rainbow what?" Drake asked.

"Serpent." The woman stood and walked through the group and took Allie's place at the door. "It's one of my favorite Dreamtime stories. Come on in. I'll introduce you to Uncle."

"You haven't introduced yourself to us yet," Geneva said.

"My name is Lenah. Come in."

Lenah pushed the door open and held it while the four people entered behind her.

Allie looked at the wide-open space. All around the perimeter of the room were displays of aboriginal culture. The far end had a platform with two dozen metal folding chairs in front of it. The main focal point of the room were two table tennis tables. At one, two teens were in the middle of a friendly game. The other was unused.

Lenah guided the group into the room and took them halfway along the side wall. There, they encountered an aboriginal man, dressed in khaki shorts and a short-sleeve shirt to match. Long, white hair, the color of snow he'd probably never seen in his life, ended just above his shoulders, and his weathered face held deep lines etched from time and experience. His eyes held the same color and brightness as Lenah's. While Lenah's choice of reading fare had been a novel, the man, who hadn't noticed their approach until Lenah spoke, preferred a newspaper.

"Uncle, these are the people from the hotel," Lenah said.

The elder let go of the newspaper and it dropped to the floor near the side of his chair. "Thank you, Roo."

"Please, Uncle, you embarrass me with that name."

The man studied her for a moment and broke into a hearty laugh. "You're right, Lenah. I'm sorry. You've grown into a woman and are certainly too old to be my Roo. You may go."

Lenah took her leave, but no one in the group stepped

forward. The elder put the chair upright and stood.

"I am Jarli. You are the people Kimberly sent over?"

Allie nodded and moved toward him, offering her hand. "I'm Allie."

Jarli put his hands in the air. "I'm sorry. In my culture, we only shake hands at funerals."

Allie dropped her hand. "I'm sorry. I meant no disrespect."

Jarli waved her off. "Think nothing of it. For you, it is a cultural norm, for me it is not. It's as simple as that, and nothing to be sorry for. So, please. What's can I do for you?"

Ingrid moved to Allie's side. "I'm Ingrid. Could you tell us anything about these symbols?" she said as she held up her phone, showing him the photo she'd snapped.

"May I?" Jarli asked.

Ingrid passed her phone to Jarli, and he studied the image on it silently for almost a full minute. He passed it back, a look of anger passed over his face like the oncoming of a summer storm.

"We don't like treasure hunters here. Go home. Go back to where you're from." Jarli growled.

"We're not treasure hunters. We're geocachers," Drake said.

"What's that?" Jarli asked.

"It's like a game. We're taking part in a geocaching contest sponsored by a group here in Alice Springs. We search for things other people have hidden."

"Like what?"

"Like whatever. Plastic boxes, film canisters, pill bottles. Whatever. We found a hint to a geocache at the same place we found those symbols," Drake explained.

"What did you find by this?" Jarli asked.

Ingrid went into her back pocket, pulled out the paper, and unfolded it. "Here. This cipher I figured out gave us the coordinates to the next part of the game."

Jarli took the sheet and studied it for a moment and passed it back. "Do you know where this goes?"

Ingrid turned the sheet around, entered the coordinates into her cell phone, and displayed a map. "Here," she said, showing him the location.

"There's nothing there but desert. Sand and stone. That's all."

"The event organizers would have placed something temporary for us to find. Like with this paper. They built a tiny pyramid from river rock, and placed a plastic box in it," Geneva said.

Allie got out her phone, brought up her geocaching app, and looked for something nearby. "Good. Mr. Jarli, would you take a walk with me?"

Jarli nodded and gestured toward the door.

"We'll be right back," Allie said. "We're only going right outside."

Allie led Jarli from the building and found Lenah back on the bench with her nose in the book. Allie checked her phone, walked away from the door ten feet and turned around and headed twenty feet in the other direction. She pivoted and came back to the bench.

"Does this geo-thing involve walking in circles?" Jarli asked.

Allie smiled, then dropped to her knees and peered under the bench.

"Would you like me to move?" Lenah said, closing her book.

Allie didn't answer. Instead, she reached for something. She stood and dropped a tiny white object into Jarli's hand.

"What's this?" Jarli asked.

"It's called a nano cache. Open it. The top screws off."

Jarli unscrewed the container, turned it over, and a tiny piece of paper fell into his hand. Intrigued, he unrolled the paper. "What are these?"

"Names of the people who have found this geocache, along with the date they found it. So, since I found this geocache, I would add my name to that paper and log it on a website."

"Did you know this was here?" Jarli asked Lenah.

"No, Uncle."

"How long has this been here?"

Allie checked her app to get the information. "Just over four years."

Jarli shook his head and handed the paper and nano back to Allie. "Who would have figured this thing has been there this whole time?"

Allie put the cache back together, then secreted it away back under the bench. Lenah returned to her book, and Allie and Jarli entered the building and found Drake playing table tennis against Ingrid and Geneva. When Drake spotted the pair, he put the ball under his paddle and returned to the barber chair.

"Well? Was it on the bench?" Drake asked.

Allie nodded.

"Okay," Jarli said. "I believe your story."

"Why did you think we were treasure hunters?" Drake asked.

"For as far back as the story of the Rainbow Serpent has been told, the *balanda* has been searching for its treasure."

"*Balanda*?" Drake asked.

"Sorry. That's our word for a white person. No offense meant."

"Is there really a treasure?" Ingrid asked.

"Come with me," Jarli said. He led the group across the room and stopped at a mosaic wall depicting an enormous snake, shaped and colored like a rainbow. At its head and tail were lakes. "In the Dreamtime stories, the Rainbow Serpent plays an important part. It came to Earth from the sky, and it created not only water, but all life associated with water. The Serpent also created land and diversity for my people. Part of the story said that the Rainbow Serpent tried to eat a kangaroo. But it failed and expelled the kangaroo and created Uluru in the process."

"Wait. A giant snake tried to eat a giant kangaroo, and it

threw up and the kangaroo turned into a mountain?" Drake asked.

"Basically, yes," Jarli said. "Another story says that the Rainbow Serpent also tried to ingest part of the earth, and from that act, the Serpent created a powerful stone in its stomach. It's said that stone could cause great chaos and hold dominion over all life."

"You think the treasure hunters you speak of are after that stone?" Ingrid asked.

"Yes," Jarli said. "Can you imagine what it would be worth? Priceless. It would be priceless. Even worse, it's said if the stone gets disturbed by human hands, the Serpent's curse will disturb the balance of nature, and it will have dire consequences all across the land."

"We can all assure you, Jarli, we have no intention of going for the Rainbow Serpent's stone," Allie said. "All we want to do is win the geocaching competition that we're in."

Jarli nodded and smiled. "Then I wish you good luck with your competition."

"Thank you, Mr. Jarli," Allie said.

Jarli smiled again. "Please, call me Uncle."

* * *

"Do you know what I've been wondering?" Geneva asked.

"When we're going to get there and if there will be a bathroom when we do?" Drake answered.

Geneva glanced over at Drake, who was sitting in the seat beside her. She squeezed his hand and smiled. "No, Sweetie, but you were close. I wondered if any of you thought it seemed a little too coincidental that the coordinates to this stage were only a few feet away from those symbols on the wall."

"Huh, I've been thinking about that, too. Was it also coincidence that one of the symbols on that wall was also on the ground where I found that first set of coordinates?" Allie said.

"And why bring Allie into the competition?" Drake asked.

"Because I'm an exceptional geocacher." Allie answered. "Obviously."

"You are," Drake conceded. "But why would a local geocaching group go through the expense of bringing in only seven teams of geocachers, five of which teams were from four other countries on the other side of the world? I'm sure there are plenty of Australian teams that could have competed."

"That competition we met at in Arizona only had ten teams," Geneva said.

"True," Drake said. "But it was still open to any geocacher in the U.S. to enter. It was only by luck of the draw that our two teams happened to be two out of the ten. So we're back to why did they want Allie?"

"She told you. She's an exceptional geocacher," Ingrid said.

Drake removed his hand from Geneva's long enough to scratch his chin. "I think maybe it's the notoriety. We were all over the papers after our adventures in Boston and Italy. Perhaps they wanted someone with name recognition?"

Ingrid stopped the car. "We're here."

Everyone got out of the Jeep and looked around. As Uncle Jarli had said, there was nothing around except rock and scrub brush.

"What did the cipher say, Ingrid?" Geneva asked.

"From where X marks the spot, go three hundred paces. North, south, east, or west?" Ingrid read aloud from the note.

"Where's the X?" Drake asked.

"I stopped right on the coordinates," Ingrid said. "Wait." Ingrid got back in the car and pulled forward a few feet. When she rejoined her friends, she saw a three-foot-high white painted X on the ground.

"Which way do we go?" Drake asked.

"It didn't say. It just gave the compass directions," Ingrid said.

"How long is a pace?" Geneva asked.

"Three feet," Drake answered.

"You sound sure."

Drake shrugged. "I read it on the Internet once. Which way is north?"

Geneva checked the compass on her phone and gestured. Drake waved, then started walking.

"East, south, and west," Geneva said, pointing out each direction on the compass.

Rather than discuss which direction to go, each of the three women picked one at random and began counting off paces.

* * *

Drake sat in the passenger seat, all the doors open to increase the air circulation, sipping on a bottle of water. He had spent the last five minutes watching someone coming from the east, trudging across the hard-packed earth, and as they got a few yards closer, he realized based on the walk it was Ingrid.

Ingrid waved, and Drake returned it. From the back of the Jeep, he retrieved a bottle of water for her, then got back in his seat and waited. Ingrid gave him a half-hearted wave when she got to within five feet of him, and in reply, Drake held out the bottle. Ingrid unscrewed the cap, and emptied the contents in one long drink, then recapped the bottle and belched.

Drake laughed. "I can see why Allie likes you so much."

Ingrid smirked. "It's one of my more appealing traits. Why didn't you come and pick me up when you saw me?"

"No keys."

Ingrid ran her hands over her pockets, then pulled the Jeep keys from her right rear pocket and held them up. "Sorry. I've been doing so well at leaving them in the car. I got the coordinates."

"Hey, I did, too." Drake said. "Why don't we go rescue the other two?"

Ingrid nodded and got behind the wheel, spun the car around, and drove west. Within two minutes, they had Geneva in sight.

"Need a lift?" Ingrid asked as she pulled up alongside.

Geneva rolled her eyes, then climbed into the backseat.

Ingrid did a U-turn, headed back to the painted X, then turned south. She drove slowly, weaving her way around large rocks and trees, all while trying to keep a southern trajectory. After three minutes, she slowed, then stopped.

"What's up?" Drake asked.

"We should have found her by now. Three hundred paces is only nine-hundred feet. Surely, we've come farther than that already."

Drake studied the scenery outside the window and saw no sign of his friend. "Turn around and go back slowly."

Ingrid completed a slow U-turn, and followed her own tire tracks, creeping along at a just over an idle. While Ingrid looked ahead, Drake and Geneva each scanned the landscape outside of their respective sides of the car.

"Stop!" Drake said.

Ingrid slammed on the brakes, but since they were going the same speed as an average walk, Drake was out of the car before the Jeep stopped rolling.

Drake made a straight line toward a U-shaped cluster of a dozen boulders, each six-feet tall, positioned like teeth in a lower jaw. As he approached the opening, he heard his name.

"Allie? Is that you?"

He stopped and listened. Her voice sounded distant. Drake took another step into the rocks and heard his name again.

"Allie?"

Drake moved closer another two feet and halted. He stood four feet in front of the boulders at the back of the U. Before him, he spotted carvings on the stone.

"Allie?"

"Drake. I'm in a hole. Help me."

Drake inched forward until he found a depression in the dirt where there was a hole the approximate size of a sewer opening. He got on his stomach and peered over the edge. He spotted Allie about six feet down.

"We've been looking for you," Drake said. "Are you hurt?"

"Not really," Allie said. "The fall shocked me more than injured me. Can you get me out of here, please?"

Drake slid forward until he could reach down into the hole. He reached his right arm as far as he could. "Grab on," he said. Allie easily reached for his arm and grabbed his forearm with both hands. "I'm ready."

Drake grunted and pulled. He lifted his arm as much as he could. "Climb up however you can. Hurry! I'm losing my grip." Drake grunted again and pulled his arm up a little more.

Allie stretched and put her left hand around Drake's neck, then reached with her right and wedged her hand under his armpit. She placed her feet against the walls of the hole and shoved, which got her torso above ground level. Drake reached down, put a hand on her butt, and boosted her up. A moment later, Allie was free of the hole, laying on Drake's prone body.

"Um, do I need to come back later?" Geneva said.

Allie looked up and saw Geneva, arms crossed, right toe tapping, creating little clouds in the dirt with each hit.

"Um, no. There was…"

"Hush and grab my hand." Geneva reached down and helped Allie to her feet.

Allie checked her pocket, pulled her phone from it, and activated it. "Good. Not broken. I got pictures of the carvings before I had my minor mishap. Did one of you manage to find the coordinates to the next stop?"

Geneva sighed. "Actually, all three of us did."

"You each found them? Are they all the same?"

"No. Apparently we've got something else to figure out," Geneva said. "Honestly, I'm growing weary of this chase."

CHAPTER NINE

"Have you found anything yet?" Ingrid asked.

"Nope," Allie said. Allie was working at the desk, and Ingrid was lying on her stomach on the bed.

"It's going to be impossible finding out any information like this unless we get some help," Ingrid said.

A moment later, a heavy knock hit the door in a rhythmic cadence.

"I got it," Allie said as she rose from her chair.

She moved to the door and opened it without checking who was on the other side.

"Here," Drake said. "Ask and ye shall receive."

Drake passed Allie a sheet of paper, and Allie took a peek at it. On it, they had listed all the teams currently in the competition with their real names and their geocaching nicknames.

"How did you get this?" Allie asked.

Drake shrugged. "I asked. I told Aussie we wanted to friend all the other players, so he had it to me within twenty minutes."

"Thanks, Drake. I'm impressed. Do you want to come in and help us search for these people online?"

"I would, but Geneva is waiting for me out by the pool. You should come and join us."

"The pool's open this late?" Allie asked.

"Yeah. They say until eleven, but I think we can squeeze out more time if we're nice and quiet," Drake said. He grinned, then raised his eyebrows twice in quick succession and added in an exaggerated wink for good measure.

Allie waved him off. "Oh, gross, Drake. You go on. You two have the time of your lives."

Drake waved goodbye and Allie shut and locked the door behind him before moving to the bed and handing Ingrid the list.

"Here, this should make things easier for us."

Ingrid took the list, scanned it, then folded the paper and tore it in half at the fold. She held out half to Allie.

Allie glanced at it. "Are you sure this is fair? You only gave me three teams. You took more than half."

Ingrid laughed. "Yeah, but I also took our team and the Canadians. I know we're not a problem, and since the Canadians are out of the competition, I won't bother looking them up, either."

Allie moved back to the desk and checked the first names on the list, which turned out to be the German team. She brought up the main geocaching website on her cell phone. There, she used the geocaching nicknames provided by Aussie to bring up the profiles of each member of the Germans. The profiles gave her a myriad of information since all of the geocachers had opened up all their geocaching information to the public. From that she mined data regarding when they started geocaching, how many geocaches each cacher had found, and, based on the maps they had, how much area they covered.

When she finished collecting geocaching statistics on the Germans, she ran through the same exercise with both Australian teams Ingrid had given her. After getting as much geocaching related information that she could, Allie opened her search, and entered one name after another into the search bar of her browser. On a pad of hotel-branded stationery, she jotted down any notes of interest as she came across them.

An hour later, Allie shut down her phone and put it on the charger. She looked over at Ingrid, who was paging through a tourist magazine of the Alice Springs area.

"Did you give up already?" Allie asked. "No luck?"

Ingrid looked at her, then held up her half of the sheet. "I finished fifteen minutes ago. I'm waiting for you."

Allie grabbed all her notes and laid down on the bed next to Ingrid. She spread the sheets out in front of her and tried to decide where to start.

"The Germans are by far the most prolific team here. Between the four of them, they have over seventy-thousand finds across all seven continents," Allie said. "As a team or as single geocachers, magazines or news articles have featured them at one time or another. Anna Vogel, who is an environmental scientist, has a social media channel with over a million subscribers. From what I could tell, the majority of her videos are half about how to save the planet, and the other half revolve around geocaching in remote places, such as the Black Forest mountains in Germany, or the fjords of Norway."

"Oh, yeah?" Ingrid said.

"I thought you'd be interested in that. I'm sure you'll get a lot of enjoyment out of those videos. Moving on to the two Australian teams you gave me. One seems relatively normal. On the team of four, they have an average of about ten thousand finds a piece, mostly around Australia and New Zealand. A couple of the members visited California recently and went up to Nevada to do a couple power trails. The team of three seems to be pretty light in their geocaching credentials. The most finds anyone among them has is three hundred, and those are all clustered around the Sydney area."

"Let me guess," Ingrid said, "They have interesting skill

sets."

Allie checked her notes. "One is a rescue diver, and the other two own a boat salvage operation. How did you know that?"

"Well, it turns out our fellow Americans are about the same. Low geocaching numbers, that look made up in some cases."

"Made up how?" Allie asked.

"On the same day, two of them found geocaches in Maine, Texas, and Washington state."

Allie shrugged. "That's possible."

Ingrid nodded. "Sure. Possible, yet highly improbable. To me it looks like they were padding their stats and they transposed some numbers or got a geocache ID wrong, which caused them to log the incorrect caches."

"What do they do for work?" Allie asked.

"I couldn't find anything out about two of them. Caleb Johnson runs a dive company that specializes in shipwreck sites in the Great Lakes, specifically Michigan."

"So there are two teams with little geocaching experience, but are good in the water?" Allie said.

Ingrid nodded. "Seems that way."

"What about the English team?" Allie asked.

"They are just what you would expect them to be. Fairly high number of finds, mostly located within England and throughout Europe. They look legit."

"Any mention of them in the media?" Allie asked.

"Only Jamie Parker. He's a teacher and uses things like geocaching to help with his teaching. He also has a channel like your German friend. Jamie doesn't have a million followers, but he seems to do okay. The impression I get from his geocaching videos is that he makes them more for his own enjoyment than he does for fame or fortune."

"Huh," Allie said. "Perhaps we should have looked up our hosts as well."

Ingrid smiled. "Already done. They all seem to be who they

say they are. They all have respectable geocaching numbers, and there is a formal geocaching group up here, although they only formalized it a couple of years ago. Aussie is a tour guide. Jake is an auto mechanic at a shop about a mile from here. Zeke is a liaison officer with works with the Indigenous community, and Ben works for the local land management department."

"I hate to say it, but Drake might be right about how they chose the teams. At least one person on every team had some sort of online exposure," Allie said.

"Sure. But what about those two outliers?" Ingrid asked.

"I don't know. That's something we'll have to figure out. I'm still not convinced that everything is on the up and up here," Allie said.

"So, now what? Should we go join Drake and Geneva at the pool?" Ingrid asked.

"Not on your life. Besides. We need to figure out where that next set of coordinates takes us," Allie said.

"You mean three sets," Ingrid said. "While you were stuck in the hole, Geneva, Drake, and I each came back with different numbers."

"You sure?" Allie said.

Ingrid got up from the bed and moved to the desk, where she had a little pile of items she'd pulled from her pockets. Among them were three slips of paper, each the size of a business card. Ingrid grabbed them and carried them back to Allie. Allie scanned the three sheets and set them on the bed next to her.

"These coordinates don't make sense," Allie said. "Just looking at them, I can tell they're not around here. I can tell just by looking at it that this one is somewhere close to Antarctica." Allie picked up the paper and turned it around so Ingrid could see it.

Ingrid studied the paper, and since the southern coordinates contained all zeros, she guessed Allie was right. She took the other two slips from Allie and entered the coordinates into her phone.

"This one's in Hawaii, and this one will take us to India," Ingrid said once she'd determined the locations of the numbers. "You know what this seems like to me?"

"We need to do a triangulation?" Allie said, way ahead of her. "Read me the numbers."

Ingrid did as asked, and Allie entered them into a tool that took the three compass points and determined the location of a single point based on the three given sets of coordinates. When the app spit out the coordinates, Allie rattled them off and Ingrid wrote them down.

"Looks like a spot a little over three hours from here, provided your tool is correct," Ingrid said, turning her phone around so Allie could look at the app.

Allie took her phone and zoomed in on the coordinates. "Watarrka National Park?"

Ingrid nodded. "That's what it looked like to me, too. Should we go tell the lovebirds?"

Allie checked the time on her phone and saw it was fifteen minutes after eleven. "No. I'm sure they're busy now."

* * *

Allie and Ingrid sat, waiting patiently in the lobby for Drake and Geneva to arrive. Fifteen minutes after their assigned meeting time, the couple came into the lobby, holding hands, and Drake with a crazy grin on his face.

"Good morning?" Ingrid asked, adding a lilt and pause on the end to make it an obvious question rather than a statement.

"How did you guess?" Drake said. He pointed at the bakery bag sitting on Ingrid's chair. "Cronut?" Drake reached for the bag without waiting for an answer, opened it, and pulled the pastry out from within. He broke it in half and gave Geneva the bigger piece.

"Did you figure out where we're headed?" Geneva asked between bites.

"Sure did, and it's a short three-hour drive away, so any time y'all are ready to saddle up, we can go," Allie said.

The four gathered their gear and headed out the hotel's back door, and as Drake reached the Jeep, he slid the backpack from his shoulder and placed it on the ground.

"We won't be leaving anytime soon," he said. "We've got a flat tire here."

"Then we have a matched pair," Ingrid said. "There's one on this side, too."

Drake sighed. "One I could fix, since we have a spare. Two will be a problem. You must've run over something in the desert."

"I doubt it was Ingrid's driving," Allie said. She went to the front flat tire by the driver's side. She bent over, and from the rubber extracted a screwdriver. Allie tossed it to Drake, and to her surprise, he caught it in midair. "Unless, of course, she ran over a toolbox and none of us noticed."

While Ingrid headed into the hotel to call for help, Drake and Allie checked over the rest of the vehicle. Drake inspected the remaining two tires, while Allie popped the hood and looked at the engine.

"Are you missing a spark plug?"

Allie turned around and spotted a mechanic standing next to a wrecker truck wearing denim overalls. He looked vaguely familiar to her, but she couldn't place the face.

"Allie, right? From Nashville?"

"That's right. You're…"

"Jake. I'm one of the hosts for this event."

Allie smiled. "Of course. Shouldn't you be out monitoring the participants?"

"I should be, but I got called into work. One of the other mechanics called in sick, so I have to do half a day to pick up the slack. But since you've found yourself in a spot of trouble, I can do both jobs at once. You've got a flat tire, I hear."

"Two of them, actually. Where'd you hear I had a flat?" Jake pointed toward the hotel. "From your friend inside."

Allie glanced at the hotel, then back at Jake. "I find it hard to believe that Ingrid, who has barely been inside long enough for the door to close behind her, has managed to call for help and have you arrive mere seconds later."

"Pure coincidence, I assure you. I was a block away when I got the call. I'd barely hung up the phone when I pulled into the parking lot. So, now, let's see what we got here so we can get you back out on the road."

Jake checked the tire closest to him first, then walked around to the other flat. "Run over something?" he asked.

"This," Drake said, handing Jake the screwdriver, "someone embedded into the sidewall. No way we could have run over that."

Jake took the screwdriver, studied it for a moment, then shoved it into his back pocket. "I'd agree. I think the easiest thing to do would be for me to run and get you a couple more tires. Shop's not far away. I'll be back in a jiffy."

Jake nodded, then climbed into his wrecker and pulled out of the driveway.

"Any of that seem suspicious to you?" Drake asked as the pair watched the brake lights of the wrecker flash and the truck turn onto the road.

"Only everything," Allie said.

"What are you guys talking about?" Ingrid asked as she approached the Jeep.

"The mechanic," Allie said. "He seemed to get here pretty quickly."

"Wait, he was here already? They told me over the phone it would be at least an hour," Ingrid said.

Forty minutes later with two new tires, the group was on the road. Ingrid behind the wheel as usual, with Geneva in the passenger seat and Drake and Allie in the back. From Alice Springs, Ingrid drove due west on State Highway 6, which was a two-lane paved road. On either side, the red sands of the Outback threatened to overtake the lonely highway, hoping to erase the scar that man had added to the terrain.

For three hours Ingrid drove, the scenery not changing much from the endless red rocks and scrub trees as they put kilometers behind them, save for the two small towns they passed.

"Can we pull over there?" Geneva asked, spotting a service station.

Without answering, Ingrid pulled up to a pump and turned off the car. "You have the card?" she asked Allie.

Allie dipped into her pocket and retrieved the credit card given to them at the beginning of the trip. "Right here. I'll get the gas."

Relieved at the news, Ingrid left the Jeep and followed Geneva and Drake into the station. Allie moved to the pump, inserted the credit card, then waited for the pump to accept the information, then added gas to the thirsty vehicle. As she waited, Allie walked a few feet away and leaned against a support pillar that held up a large tin-roof above the pumps to keep them shaded. She closed her eyes for a moment, and she opened them as another vehicle pulled in to the station. Allie spotted Will and Jamie in the front seat of their Land Rover as Jamie pulled up to a pump of his own.

Allie moved back to hers, hoping to avoid conversation and slip into the restroom, but the pump kept feeding the Jeep.

"Amy! I thought that was you!"

Allie exhaled, turned around, and spotted Liz headed in her direction.

"Can you believe the ride out here, Amy?"

"It's Allie, actually. Not Amy."

"Sorry. And you'll never believe what happened to us. We

were all ready to start out this morning, and we had three flat tires. Can you imagine that? It took us forever to get on the road this morning."

"Oh, sorry. What happened?" Allie asked.

"I don't know. You can ask one of the men. I need to run inside."

"Don't know," Jamie said as he reached for his pump. "That Jake was right on top of it, though, and got us back on the road fairly quick. Only about an hour behind schedule."

"Let me guess," Allie said. The pump finally shut off, so Allie returned the nozzle and closed her gas cap. "He just happened to be driving by and was there to help you within a couple minutes of you needing it?"

Jamie lifted his hat, then wiped his brow with his forearm before replacing his cap. "Yeah. How did you know that?"

Allie shrugged. "Lucky guess."

CHAPTER TEN

Ingrid pulled into the parking area of King's Canyon, found a spot among the crowded lot, and shut down the Jeep.

"I guess we're walking from here," Ingrid said, noticing the pink line on her GPS expected them to go well past the parking area.

"How far?" Drake asked.

"The direct line says it's a little over a mile from here," Geneva said. "But based on the terrain, I'm guessing it's a little longer."

Allie grabbed her backpack, pulled a bottle of water from the case and shoved the bottle into the mesh holder on the side of her backpack. Rather than ask if anyone needed a bottle, she handed them out to Drake, Geneva, and Ingrid, who all accepted them without question and stowed them away.

"All right, Geneva. Lead the way," Allie said as she closed the Jeep's rear door.

The group walked a few feet to the edge of the parking lot leading to the trail, where they found an informational sign.

"That's cool," Drake said.

The sign, made of wood, was one found at parks all over the world advising potential hikers what they were getting into. This one not only encouraged travelers to drink plenty of water but also warned of the dangers of walking in high temperatures. Unlike most informational signs, this one contained a scale on it that ran from five degrees to forty-five degrees Celsius with a sliding bar on top that a ranger could move to tell hikers the projected temperature ranges for the day.

"Are we taking the canyon or the creek walk trail?" Drake asked, reading the signs that pointed toward the trails. "Please tell me it's the creek trail." The creek walk looked half as short and took a quarter of the time as the longer canyon trail.

"They both start in the same place, so I can't tell you that," Geneva said. "Come on, lazy bones."

Geneva tugged at the shoulder of Drake's shirt and pulled him toward the trail. They walked in no big hurry for three-tenths of a mile and arrived at another sign. This one listed four trails with directional arrows pointing to each one. The creek walk and canyon walk distances dropped by a half kilometer, but the times were the same. The red arrow for the creek trail and the blue arrow for the canyon rim trail varied slightly, and a hundred feet up the path, the trail split into two.

"Well?" Drake asked, shifting his feet like an impatient puppy.

Geneva studied her GPS for a moment, then took a brief look at the sign. "It looks like we'll be on the creek walk."

"Yes!" Drake said, pumping his fist in the air. From where they stood, the creek walk was only two kilometers, with a completion estimate of one hour. "Let's do this!" Without waiting, Drake grabbed Geneva's hand and began powerwalking to the start of the creek trail.

"Hey, slow down," Geneva said. "There's no rush."

Drake dropped his speed by half a step, but that was it, and he dragged Geneva on a pace that left Ingrid and Allie literally in the dust.

"Should we go faster?" Ingrid asked as the pair watched their companions rush along the trail.

"Nope," Allie said. "Give him like three hundred yards and he'll tire and slow down on his own."

"Unless Geneva stops him first," Ingrid said.

Allie checked behind them to see if there were other hikers on the trail, and, seeing no one, reached over and took Ingrid's hand.

"It's a beautiful day," Allie said, looking up into the cornflower blue sky, unmarked by clouds or so much as a bird in flight.

Ingrid squeezed Allie's hand but didn't respond. She didn't need to. The pair were just as comfortable with silence as they were in conversation. Four-hundred million years of weather and erosion flattened the bedrock to a somewhat bumpy but well-used path that led the group from the parking area into a canyon through which a river flowed slow and steady, even in the arid climate. The water stayed near the center of the banks, a sign that they were in the middle of the dry season.

"Hey, look at that," Ingrid said, breaking the silence. She pointed to a nearby rock where there was an eight-inch lizard lying on a rock in the sun.

Allie followed Ingrid's finger and spotted the reptile rocking a coat of camouflaged desert browns and a tan that faded to a light green. Unlike other species of lizards she'd seen, this one looked like it had been a part of a science experiment gone wrong, as it had protruding spines that made the creature look like it was cross-bred with a rosebush.

"He's a cutie, isn't he?" Allie asked.

"Adorable," Ingrid agreed. "Come on, they're waiting for us."

Allie pulled her eyes away from the lizard and focused farther up the trail. It followed a bend in the river, and she spotted Geneva and Drake waiting for them two hundred yards ahead. Even at that distance, Allie could tell Geneva seemed frustrated with something dealing with her GPS, and Drake had found a seat on a nearby boulder.

Ingrid and Allie picked up the pace and joined their friends within five minutes. By the time they got to them, Geneva had tucked her GPS back in her pocket, and Drake was tossing pebbles into the water.

"Waiting for us?" Ingrid asked.

"Didn't have a choice. We've hit the end of the road here," Geneva said.

"What do you mean?" Ingrid asked. "Don't we stay on the trail?" Ingrid pointed ahead and to the right, where the trail followed the canyon wall and veered away from the river.

Geneva fished her GPS from her pocket and held it up so Ingrid and Allie could see the screen. "According to this, we're only fifty feet away, but in that direction." Geneva pointed to where the river was flowing out from a hole in the canyon wall.

"Did you follow the trail to see if it loops back in that direction?" Allie asked.

"It doesn't," Drake said, tossing another pebble into the river. It struck a boulder and rebounded, landing near his feet. "I followed it for a few hundred yards, but it seems to curl back around to where we came from."

Allie took the machine from Geneva, looked at the screen, and took a step toward the river. The canyon walls sloped inward, and the water lazily trickled from a four-foot-wide gap that resembled the narrow end of a funnel.

"Maybe we have to go up," Drake said, tossing a stone at the canyon wall.

Allie looked above her. Although she wasn't the best at estimating heights and distances, she guessed the climb would be at least fifty feet to the top. "I'm not climbing up there."

"Perhaps we should have taken the other trail. Doesn't that

go to the top?" Ingrid asked.

"I don't think it comes this way," Geneva answered. "I'm pretty sure it follows the larger canyon to the west."

Allie grunted, scratched her head, and took another step toward where the river came out of the wall. The water dropped from a shelf that was waist high to Allie before continuing on its journey to wherever it eventually ended up. She stepped as close to the shelf's center as she could without getting wet, and peered into the crevice from which the water spilled. She leaned forward and took a closer look. From her position, she swore she saw light coming from the other end.

"Maybe we need to go in," Allie said. Without waiting for a response from anyone, she boosted herself onto the ledge with her hands and stood, wiping her dusty palms on her pants as she did so.

Allie heard Ingrid calling her name behind her, but she ignored it and shuffled forward through the tunnel, happy that the river wasn't any higher. If it were, she wouldn't have been able to enter and would probably have gotten ejected by the force of the water. She had to crouch the closer she got to the end, but after four feet of walking unnaturally, she came through to the other end of the tunnel and was once again in the sunlight. Allie looked up and noticed she was at the bottom of a natural well, the cliff walls extending up in almost a perfect circle, and above her was the wisp of a white cloud and bright blue sky.

She turned her attention to level ground. To her right, there was a hole in the wall that the river ran from, which was no more than eighteen inches high and five feet wide. Before her, and to her left, were two additional caverns. The one in front was tall enough for an eight-foot person to walk into, and the one on the left was just over half that tall.

"There you are."

Allie turned and saw Drake coming out of the tunnel.

"This is impressive," Drake said, stopping and looking over

the area. "Do you think we need to go into one of those tunnels?"

"Probably."

Allie and Drake turned around when they heard voices coming from the tunnel. They expected to see Geneva and Ingrid, but also coming through were the four members of the English team.

"Amy," Liz said, holding her arms open, expecting a hug, as she approached Allie. "I can't believe that we found you."

"Yeah. It's amazing," Allie said.

"What do we have here?" Will said, stepping past Allie and Drake. He crouched to look into the tunnel to the left and took a few feet into the tunnel ahead. "Jamie, which way?"

Jamie referenced his phone, stepped toward one mouth, and then the next. "I can't get a good reading down here. I think it's the walls making my signal bounce."

"What do you blokes have, then?" Will asked.

Before Allie said anything, Geneva checked her GPS and offered the same analysis that Jamie did.

"Well then, we should divide up these two tunnels and see where they lead. Come on, now," Will said, taking a step toward the larger tunnel.

"Hold on there a second," Drake said. The muscles in his neck tightened as he took a step toward Will. "We got here first. Shouldn't we get to choose which tunnel we want to explore?"

Jamie stepped in front of Will, a scowl appearing on his face.

Allie had been in enough situations where the male ego overrode emotions, so to tamp things down a bit, she got in front of Drake and put a hand on his chest.

"It's okay, Drake. There's plenty of room for all of us here. If they want to go that way, let them. Come on. Let's go."

Drake held his position for an extended second, then capitulated and turned toward the smaller tunnel. "Who has the flashlight?"

Ingrid produced it from her pack, and without waiting,

clicked it on, bent over, and walked into the opening with Drake a step behind her.

"After you," Allie said to Geneva.

Without a response, Geneva stepped into the opening. Allie gave the team from England a smile, took a deep breath, exhaled, and followed Geneva into the void.

Allie had to crouch through a hundred yards of the tunnel, then move forward on hands and knees. She kept a steady pace and stopped when she felt a hand on her shoulder.

"You can get up now," Drake said.

Allie looked up but saw nothing but darkness. "What's going on?"

"My flashlight batteries died," Ingrid said.

Before Allie could respond, a bright light appeared on her face and blinded her.

"Sorry," Geneva said, moving the light and focusing it on Ingrid instead, who was rummaging through her backpack for a fresh set of batteries.

A few seconds later, Ingrid's light came back to life, and she swept the beam on the surrounding walls. They stood in an oval-shaped room, thirteen feet long and six feet wide. At the far end were six stalactites and five stalagmites that gave the cave's end an appearance like that of a gaping maw waiting to chew up and swallow anyone who got near. Ingrid shined the flashlight throughout the room, disturbing an insect that skittered away into the darkness, but finding nothing else.

"Dead end. I guess we should have picked the other cave," Drake said.

"May I?" Allie asked Ingrid as she held out her hand.

Ingrid handed over the flashlight and Allie moved to the other end of the room where she focused on the speleothems, inspecting the fronts of the geologic features. When she moved around the stalagmite on her far left, she noticed something odd.

"Hey, Drake, I need some muscle over here," Allie said.

Drake joined Allie and she pointed at a stone that looked like a four-foot-diameter marble.

"Can you move that?" Allie asked.

Drake shrugged, then pushed all his weight against the stone. It didn't budge. He stepped back and shook his head. "There's no way."

"There must be. Someone has moved it before," Allie said, pointing to a spot of scuffed ground where the rock had been.

"There is," Ingrid said, stepping to the rock. She looked around, spotted a smaller rock, gathered it up and placed it a foot away from the boulder. Off in the room's corner, she found a hearty piece of wood as tall as her.

"What are you doing?" Drake asked.

"Haven't you ever heard that Archimedes quote that if you give me a lever long enough and a fulcrum on which to put it, I can move the world?" Ingrid asked.

Ingrid shoved the wood under the boulder, placed it on top of the fulcrum, and pushed. The boulder moved an inch and then stopped.

"You want to help me out here?" Ingrid asked.

Drake traded places with her, and he pushed down on the lever and the boulder rolled half a foot.

Allie bent over and shined the flashlight into the space behind the boulder. "There's an opening here. We need to move that rock farther away."

Drake handed Ingrid the lever, repositioned the fulcrum, and with another push, rolled the boulder far enough to expose the opening.

"That's good enough," Allie said. She bent over and shined the flashlight into the hole. "There's a room in there."

"Are you going in?" Ingrid asked.

Allie shined the light around the small opening. She knew she could fit, but hesitated, knowing the walls would compress as soon as she entered because of her claustrophobia.

"I got this," Geneva said, stepping to the hole. She took the flashlight from Allie, got on her knees, then slithered into the hole like an escaping serpent.

Allie, Drake, and Ingrid held back and waited patiently for one minute. When a second minute passed without them hearing anything, Drake bent over and yelled Geneva's name. After a third minute passed, Drake got down on his belly and entered the hole. Slowly, he advanced, then stopped when only his ankles and shoes were visible to Allie and Ingrid.

"Hey. Pull me out!" Drake yelled.

"You stuck?" Allie asked.

"No. Just pull me out."

Allie and Ingrid each grabbed an ankle, and after a quick countdown, they each pulled. Inch by inch, Drake's body emerged. First his legs, then waist, then his torso, and finally his head appeared.

"Thanks," he said as he rolled over to get away from the hole.

Allie opened her mouth to ask a question, then held it when Geneva's head appeared. By the time Geneva's waist appeared, Drake was on his feet, helping her from the hole.

"Another dead end?" Allie asked.

"Oh, no. Not at all," Geneva said. From the front pocket of her jeans, she extracted her cell phone. She took a moment to bring up the gallery.

"It's a remarkable room in there. It's covered with drawings," Geneva said.

While the others clustered around her, Geneva flipped through the photos, one after another, each one containing aboriginal art.

"Hey, go back," Allie said.

Geneva stopped flipping forward and scrolled back a few frames.

"That's it. Stop."

Geneva handed her phone to Allie.

"These symbols. They're like ones we've seen before," Allie said.

Geneva smiled. "I thought you might be interested in those. I…"

She trailed off when a rumble came from deep inside the cavern. The room shifted a bit, and bits of stone and dust rained from the ceiling.

"We should leave," Geneva and Drake said in unison.

Ingrid, closest to the exit, didn't hesitate and rushed into it with Geneva, Allie, and Drake inches behind her. Within three minutes, they arrived at the entrance to the cavern. Geneva crouched, ready to follow the river back to the trail, when Drake grabbed her by the shoulder and turned her around.

"Wait," Drake said, holding out his open palm. "Give me the flashlight."

Geneva complied and Drake turned on the light and stepped into the tunnel the English team had entered. As Geneva watched Drake disappear into the dark, she noticed for the first time the fine cloud of dust still settling from outside the tunnel.

"Drake!" Geneva yelled as she attempted to follow him. Before she could, Ingrid grabbed her arm and pulled her away from the opening.

"No, Geneva. He'll be back in a minute," Ingrid said.

The trio waited until Drake appeared, covered in a fine layer of silt.

"We need to get some help out here. They're trapped," Drake said as he took off his cap and wiped the dust from his face.

"Anyone hurt?" Allie asked.

"I don't know."

Allie retrieved her phone and checked for a signal. "I've got no reception here. I'll take it outside."

Allie followed the river through the short cavern, jumped off the shelf where the water exited the rock, ran down the trail fifty yards and checked her phone. She showed no surprise when she discovered no bars. Allie let loose a long exhale, then jogged farther up the trail, stopped, checked her bars, and, not seeing any, took off running again.

The parking area was in sight by the time Allie got a single bar of reception, but she was thirsty, sore, and panting much too hard to make a call right away. Instead, she slowed her pace to a walk and made her way to the Jeep. She yanked on the passenger door, hoping to take a seat inside, and realized Ingrid had the keys. Allie let her backpack slid from her shoulders and pulled out her water bottle and drained most of it in a few gulps. She closed her eyes and forced herself to relax, and after forty-five seconds, she opened her eyes, exhaled, and made the call for help.

Allie was leaning against the rear tire of the Jeep, enjoying the shade of the vehicle, when she heard footsteps approach. She opened her eyes and saw her three friends standing before her.

"You forgot to come back," Drake said.

Allie smiled and took Drake's hand when he offered to help her up. "I didn't forget. I didn't want to walk all the way back there. Besides, I called in the professionals. What else could I do?"

"You could direct us to the next set of coordinates," Drake said.

Geneva handed Allie her phone and Allie scrolled through Geneva's pictures.

"Did you take photos of everything in that room?" Allie asked.

"Yes. Everything I could see in there," Geneva said. "Why do you ask?"

Allie handed the phone back. "Because there are no coordinates. Only more symbols."

CHAPTER ELEVEN

"What are we supposed to do with these?" Ingrid asked, perusing through the photographs that Geneva had shared within the group chat.

Allie finished running a towel through her hair. When she got back to the hotel room, feeling sweaty and gross from her run through the canyon. She'd spent a half hour under the hot water, washing her hair twice, and her body three times, before standing with her hands against the wall, letting the water pound at her shoulders and back.

"I don't have a clue. I haven't looked at them since we left the canyon," Allie said.

Allie gave the towel a last run through her hair and ran her fingers through it rather than brush it. She set the towel on the bed, then asked for Ingrid's phone. Allie moved over to the desk and sat in the chair as she enlarged and studied each of Geneva's photos. Most of them were much better representations of objects, rather than the crude stick drawings she thought of when she pictured cave drawings. She could make out several things, including people, kangaroos, various types of fish, birds, and three different types of lizards.

"I honestly don't understand what any of this tells us," Allie said, putting down the phone. "I certainly don't recognize any coordinates among them."

"Maybe Geneva missed something. Perhaps we should take a trip back there and look around a little closer."

Allie sighed and reviewed all the photos again. "I don't think she missed anything, based on the way she overlapped her photos. And there are no rocks visible to hide things behind or under, and there's certainly no large 'X' marking the spot. No. I don't think there were any coordinates there. Maybe they were in the other branch of the cave, where our English friends went."

"I hope not," Ingrid said. "I talked to Geneva while you were in the shower. Our friends from across the pond were wandering around in circles until one of them set off some booby trap that caused a cave in. Everyone got injured except that woman who always gets your name wrong. And worse, the park has shut off all access to that area, so we couldn't get back in there if we wanted to."

Allie frowned. "Is everyone going to be okay?"

"Yeah. There's a broken arm and a concussion in the group, and three out of four are staying in the hospital for observation, but they'll all survive."

Allie nodded. "That's good. But they didn't find any coordinates or anything?"

"Geneva said they found nothing at all in there. That's something I don't get. Why would they take us to a place but not have any additional coordinates to discover?" Ingrid shrugged and picked up Allie's wet towel from the bed and headed toward the bathroom.

"Why indeed?" Allie said under her breath.

Allie ran through the pictures again and rather than the kangaroos and lizards; she focused on the series of symbols present at the top and bottom of the larger images.

"You've got that look on your face," Ingrid said as she wrapped her arms around Allie from behind and gave her a hug.

"What look?"

"Where you're on the verge of an intellectual breakthrough but haven't connected all the dots yet."

Allie reached her arms back and grabbed as much of Ingrid as she could, giving her an awkward reverse hug.

"I do have a great idea. Tomorrow, first thing, we'll go over and visit Uncle Jarli."

* * *

"He's waiting for you," Lenah said without looking up from her book. She spread out across the bench, her back against one armrest, her feet propped upon the other.

"How could he be? We didn't tell anyone we were coming," Geneva said.

Lenah shrugged. "I don't know. He just told me to let you pass when you showed up this morning. You'd better go in. He doesn't like to be kept waiting."

Drake held the door open while the three women entered, Allie in front.

"Uncle Jarli," Allie said as she approached the man who was sitting in his barber chair, thumbing through a magazine.

When he saw her, he erupted into a smile, got down from the chair, and encased her in a hug.

"Good to see you again," Uncle Jarli said into her ear. "You have questions for me?"

"How did you guess?" Allie asked.

"There was a group who came by last night. Rude people. Disrespectful."

"Must have been the Germans," Drake said.

"No. I believe they came from your country," Uncle Jarli responded. "But don't you worry, I didn't give them any information, none at all. I figured you would show up this morning since you weren't here yesterday. Now. How can I help you?"

Allie opened the group chat on her phone, brought up the pictures, and handed her phone over to Uncle Jarli. "Can you tell me what these mean?"

Uncle Jarli took the phone and scrolled through the photos. He looked up for a second. "One of you, go to the desk up front and grab me a piece of paper and a pen."

Drake nodded, then retrieved the requested items and handed them to Uncle Jarli, who moved to a bookcase and placed the paper flat. As the group looked on, Uncle Jarli referenced the phone and sketched several of the symbols from the pictures onto the paper. When he finished, there were over a dozen jotted down, and he tapped the pen on the bookcase as he thought about what he saw on the page. He underlined one and drew an arrow to a different position in the sequence, then did the same with another symbol. Satisfied, he set down the pen and picked up the paper.

"Do you know what this says?" Uncle Jarli asked, then he chuckled. "You don't, of course, otherwise you wouldn't be here. This tells the tale of the legend of the Rainbow Serpent, much of which I've already told you." Uncle Jarli motioned through three-quarters of the symbols. "There is some new information here. These symbols over here allude to a waterhole that is about a hundred kilometers to the west of here."

"Are you saying that should be our next stop?" Allie asked.

"What you do is up to you. If you do head out that way, remember my warning. My people believe evil spirits haunt the area, and it's an area where people have mysteriously disappeared."

"Wait," Drake said, "what do you mean by disappear?"

"The locals stay away from the area, so tourists are the ones who usually go to the area and never return."

"Are you sure they disappear and don't just leave town?" Ingrid asked.

Uncle Jarli shrugged and raised his hands in the air. "Who am I to say? Anyway, if you do go there, heed my words and be careful."

"Where is this place exactly?" Allie asked.

Uncle Jarli nodded, then flipped over his piece of paper and began drawing a rudimentary map.

* * *

A little over two hours later, Ingrid pulled onto the shoulder of a highway, surprised to see four other vehicles lined up and spaced six feet apart from each other.

"Looks like we have company," Geneva said as Ingrid stopped the Jeep, threw it into Park, and cut the ignition. "Any chance that these are random tourists and not our fellow geocachers?"

"We won't know for sure until we get in there," Drake said as he opened the car door and exited. He stretched, then moved around to the rear door, opened it, and handed out the backpacks as each of the women joined him.

"Everyone have water?" Allie asked, holding up a bottle from the case. When everyone nodded, Allie stuffed the extra bottle in her own backpack and closed the Jeep door.

"Anyone know which way to go?" Ingrid asked.

Drake pointed at the ground in front of him. It was a mix of hard-packed earth, dirt, and sand, and within the sand were sets of fresh footprints. "Let's follow these."

Drake led the way, followed in a line by Geneva, Ingrid, and Allie. They trudged for a few hundred yards across open ground, with Drake following the footprints like a master tracker. When he lost the trail, he carried on forward until he picked it up again. After a few hundred yards, the group found themselves on the top of a bluff overlooking a circular area that looked from the top like a giant bowl.

"What happened here?" Geneva said.

"A meteor impact a billion years ago would be my guess," Drake said.

"Look over there," Ingrid said, pointing into the bowl.

"Looks like a party," Drake said.

Down in the crater, two teams had assembled together and looked to be milling about, like they were exchanging small talk at a cocktail party. The bowl had a trail that followed the side around and down, and two teams were descending, a hundred yards apart, in order to meet the others. A large waterhole made up the bowl's center.

"Looks like a party no one invited us to," Geneva said. "Should we crash it?"

Drake grinned. "I think that sounds like a great idea. All we need to do is find the trail down there and we'll crash the party."

"It's over there," Geneva said, pointing to a ramshackle, hand painted sign that read simply TRAIL, only forty feet from where they stood overlooking the bowl. The group moved to the trail, with Allie taking up the rear.

"Are you going to be okay with this?" Drake asked when he glanced down and saw the narrow path that led down the hill.

"At least there's something for me to hold on to," Allie said, eyeing a guide rope that some kind soul had attached to the wall. "I only wish I had a climbing harness. But, to answer your question, I should be fine going down this as long as I take it slow, so I'll bring up the rear."

Geneva waited while Drake moved down the trail a dozen feet and followed behind him.

"Are you sure you're up to this?" Ingrid asked, hesitating while putting some distance between herself and Geneva. "You don't have the best track record with large hills."

"Or heights," Allie added. "I think I'll be good as long as I hang onto the rope and keep my eyes right in front of me. You can go. Don't worry about waiting for me."

Ingrid took off down the trail, and Allie took hold of the guide rope and placed one foot in front of the other, concentrating her gaze on the path in front of her. Foot by foot, she descended into the crater, not bothering to check on either her progress or that of her friends. She came to a dead stop when the guide rope ended, looked up, and saw she'd reached the bottom after almost forty-five minutes of trudging ever forward.

Except for one person who was exploring on their own away from the primary group, everyone else stood gathered together. As Allie walked toward the geocachers, Geneva spotted her, broke off from the group, and met Allie halfway.

"What's going on?" Allie asked.

"Zoe's team was here first. Apparently, they found an underground tunnel system that feeds this waterhole. They tried exploring it on their own, but it's too large for just one group."

"Who's Zoe?" Allie asked.

"See that tall brunette in the black leggings who looks like she spends every waking moment playing beach volleyball?" Geneva asked, pointing to a woman wearing a sun visor and dark sunglasses currently talking with her hands to make a point neither Allie nor Geneva could hear.

"Yeah, I see her," Allie said. "Do you know what they're talking about?"

"I do. Half the teams want to go in as one group and cover as much ground as possible, then share whatever information they find with everyone else."

"The other half of the teams want to go it alone?" Allie interjected.

"Exactly," Geneva said. "We should go over and find out which it is."

The two women started walking toward the group, but had only gone a few steps before the group turned as one and headed toward a wall. Allie and Geneva followed behind, and eventually they stopped and entered the wall by getting on hands and knees and crawling through a space only a couple of feet square. One by one, the people disappeared into the hole until Geneva, Allie, and one other man remained outside.

"Not going in?" Geneva asked the man.

He grinned, then patted his belly. Not that there was one, unless you counted all his abdominal muscles that showed prominently from his shirt he wore at least one size too small. "I'm too broad in the shoulders," he said, his Australian accent more pronounced than anyone else on the continent the women had heard.

Allie looked at the opening. It seemed to get smaller the more she stared at it. "I'm not sure I can do this. I think I'm about caved out for this trip."

Geneva patted her on the back. "I understand. I'll let Drake and Ingrid know that you'll be out here waiting for us."

"Don't worry, I'll protect the little lady," the Australian hunk said.

Geneva gave him a sly smile. "It's more likely she'll have to protect you." Geneva gave Allie a nod, then dropped to her knees and scurried into the hole.

"My name's Noah. Would you like to get to know each other while we wait?"

Allie smiled, then turned away as if interested by the view and rolled her eyes.

* * *

"Allie's not coming," Geneva said to Drake and Ingrid.

Neither one expressed surprise. They each had their fears and dislikes, and everyone in their little group knew them, respected them, and only teased each about them whenever they got the opportunity.

The trio stood in a thirty-foot-round cavern with a domed roof with a half-dozen exits that left the room. Geneva scanned the area and noticed the other four teams had each picked an exit and were heading for it, leaving two to choose from.

"Well, where are we going?" Geneva asked as she extracted her flashlight from her backpack.

"Everyone decided on a random route," Drake said. "It doesn't matter which to me we go, so it's up to you. Left or right?"

"I don't care," Geneva said. "Ingrid?"

"I think we should go… to the right. I have an intuition about going right," Ingrid answered.

Drake chuckled. "Is it a feeling that we're going to find what we're looking for, or a one that we're going to be three more names on the list of people who have disappeared in here?"

Ingrid giggled. "That remains to be seen."

"Oh, well. Please, after you two," Drake said, sweeping his arms toward the entry.

Geneva kissed Drake on the cheek. "Such chivalry!"

Geneva clicked on her flashlight and entered the corridor without hesitation.

Ingrid stopped right in front of Drake. He pursed his lips, ready for a kiss, but Ingrid tapped him on the cheek instead.

"No way," Ingrid said, then jogged to catch up with Geneva.

"Hey, you can't blame me for trying," Drake said, turning to follow his friends.

Drake sauntered in behind Ingrid, following her step by step. The passageway was a yard wide and the ceiling high enough that they could walk erect through the cavern. As Drake followed Ingrid, he trained his light on the walls while he walked, finding nothing but natural rock as he did so. The cavern followed a bend in an arc to their right, then bent around to the left. Twice they entered small rooms, but since there was only one way in and out, they stopped long enough to check for any markings on the walls before moving on.

Drake's light caught a line running perfectly parallel to the wall, intersected almost in the middle with a straight line that ran from ceiling to floor. Thinking it was something important, he stopped to examine his finding. He shined his light over the area to see if there were any other markings on the wall, and finding none, he stepped closer to the wall.

"Drake, are you coming?" Ingrid asked after realizing Drake had stopped and was a good twenty feet behind him. The beam of her flashlight danced across the floor until she found Drake and put him in the spotlight.

"Yeah. Just checking something out. Keep going. You don't need to wait for me."

"You sure?" Ingrid asked.

"Yep. I'm right behind you."

The beam left Drake and spun around and bobbed forward as Ingrid turned and rushed to catch Geneva.

Drake turned his attention back to the wall. He took another step closer and leaned in until his nose practically touched the stone. He ran his fingers along the seam, found it was a naturally occurring crack in the rock, and turned away from it.

Drake headed in Ingrid's last known location and walked a full four paces before his brand new flashlight flickered and dropped out.

"Crap," Drake said in the dark. He clicked the power button a few times, then tapped the flashlight against the palm of his hand, hoping beyond reason it would suddenly come on. "Geneva! Ingrid! Wait up for me. I need to change the batteries in my flashlight."

Drake took his phone from his back pocket and turned on the flashlight. He set it on the floor and propped it against the wall, so it cast light in the widest arc possible. Drake shrugged off his backpack, set it on the ground, and rooted around in the front pocket until he found a small plastic bag containing spare batteries in a variety of sizes. He opened the flashlight, removed the old batteries and dropped them into the pocket before adding fresh batteries. The light came on the second he pressed the button, and he gathered up all his items, threw his backpack over his shoulders, and rushed to catch up with his friends.

Drake jogged down the passageway and, twenty paces later, entered a room. He expected to see Geneva and Ingrid in the vicinity but didn't. The room wasn't a large one, only six feet square at best, but it had three corridors that left the room.

Drake moved to the first and yelled for his friends, but got no answer. He did the same with the second and third, and when no one responded, he trained the flashlight on the ground and tried to pick up footprints, but the hard bedrock yielded no clues as to which way his friends headed.

"Ingrid said she had a feeling about going right, so hopefully they stuck to that," Drake said as he selected the passage just off his right shoulder.

The corridor curved to the left, straightened, and dumped him out into another room with multiple exit points. Again, he chose the right one, and walked on. After ten minutes, he entered an enormous cavern and raised his flashlight and moved the beam around the room. The space was large enough that the flashlight didn't fully illuminate the space, so Drake walked forward fifty feet until the light reached the far wall. There, he spotted a half dozen exits from the chamber, and he walked the length of the wall, finding more exits as he went. The room curved, and he followed it, mentally recording corridor after corridor.

Drake had an epiphany, stopped, and turned the flashlight in the direction from which he came. As he did, he spotted more potential exits, but nothing to show which one was his.

"Shit," Drake muttered, realizing he had gotten himself turned around and lost.

CHAPTER TWELVE

Drake slowed his pace through the room and eventually stopped. He found four fist-sized stones and stacked them in a cairn in front of the passage closest to him. With that task complete, he walked the entire perimeter, counting the passages as he did.

"Thirty," he said as he returned to the cairn. "Thirty options are twenty-nine more than I need."

Drake approached the passage with the cairn directly in front and stepped in. He followed the beam of his flashlight, and when the passage came to a dead end, he turned around and headed back to the other end. When he reached the cairn, he moved one entryway to his left and headed down the corridor. His footsteps echoed in the space before him as he rushed down the hall, only half paying attention to the walls as he hoped to find his way out. He stopped when the flashlight beam illuminated a wall before him and he realized he'd once again hit a dead end.

Drake returned to the cavern, found a rock, and placed it before the corridor he'd just investigated and discounted. He slipped his backpack from his shoulders, set it down, and removed a bottle of water from his pack, took a swig, and returned it to its spot. He placed his back on the wall and slid to a sitting position.

"Maybe I can call for help," Drake mused, sliding his phone from his pocket. He unlocked the screen and checked the bars, noticing he had zero. He exhaled and turned off his phone and shoved it back into his pocket. "Or perhaps I need to save myself."

Drake, having wallowed in enough self-pity, struggled to his feet, found another rock, and dropped it beside the passageway. He entered the corridor and followed it, sensing he was taking a large arc, that reminded him of the shape of a light bulb. The passage was a long one, and Drake moved from a walk to a shuffle, to a slow jog in order to move through it faster. After four minutes, the space opened, and he found himself in a large cavern.

He moved the flashlight over the area, and to his surprise, he spotted the cairn he built fifteen feet to his left. Between him and the cairn was a corridor that didn't have a rock in front of it, so he knew he hadn't yet explored it. He moved away from the opening, found a rock the size of a canned ham, and dropped it directly in front of the passageway he had just exited.

"So that's the way it's going to be," Drake said when he positioned the stone.

Drake entered the passage to his left and followed the trail. Rather than dead end, or take an arc, he walked straight for a quarter of a mile and made a sharp right turn. He carried on for another quarter mile, made another right turn, walked for only a few hundred yards, turned right again, and after twenty strides, entered the cavern.

"Son of a gun," Drake said as he shined his light to the left and right. He couldn't see his cairn or any of the rocks he'd placed, but the room had a familiar enough feel to it that he believed he'd once again ended up where he started from. Drake stepped into the room a few feet, found another rock, which this time resembled a dinner plate, and placed the rock by the opening. He followed the wall, and when he spotted his cairn, he breathed a little easier, knowing that if the passages were either dead ends or ones that looped around to other doors, he'd find his way out, eventually.

* * *

"I don't think it was this way," Geneva said. "I'm pretty sure we should have turned right back at that last junction."

Ingrid turned around and shined her flashlight on the corridor that they'd come down. "I don't know. This looks familiar to me."

Geneva rolled her eyes. "Of course it looks familiar. It's rock, dirt, and sand. It looks familiar because it's the exact same thing as everything else we've seen since we've been in here." She took a deep inhale and yelled. "Drake! Drake?"

Ingrid added her voice to Geneva's, calling Drake's name and then waiting for a response.

"Hold on, I think I hear something," Ingrid said, putting her hand in the air to stop Geneva.

Both women halted and cocked their heads like prairie dogs and stayed stone still for ten full seconds.

"I don't hear anything," Geneva said.

"I do. It's coming from in front of us." Ingrid pointed in the direction from which she detected the voices. "Let's go. If it's Drake, we can work our way out of this mess. If it's not Drake, then whoever it is can help us find him."

"That sounds like a plan," Geneva said. "We never should have let him out of our sight. This isn't a great place to get lost."

"Exactly what I was thinking. I'm hoping we don't run into any missing people that passed away while walking in circles, trapped in here forever."

"That won't happen."

Ingrid stopped walking and looked back. "How do you know?"

Geneva held her flashlight under her chin and grinned, giving her face a Halloween appearance. "Because if they were dead, the animals in here would have eaten them."

"That's not helpful," Ingrid said. "But, hey, thanks for giving me something else to worry about."

Geneva laughed and pointed her flashlight into the darkness beyond Ingrid. "Let's keep going."

The pair walked on and eventually came to a small room, no more than six feet square, which had two exits, one straight ahead, and one to their left.

"Which way?" Geneva asked.

"Why are you asking? I've never been in here before," Ingrid said with a slight edge to her words.

Geneva, sensing the irritation and worry in Ingrid's voice, dropped the questioning and pointed to the corridor nearest to them. "Let's go that way."

Ingrid stepped into the corridor and took a dozen steps before she stopped.

"What's up?" Geneva asked.

"I think I see light up ahead," Ingrid said. "Turn off your flashlight."

As one, they turned the flashlights off, and Ingrid strained to peer farther ahead. "It is light. Come on."

Ingrid turned her flashlight back on and picked up her pace. She rushed forward twenty feet and realized the ceiling height was getting lower. Moving on, eventually she needed to crouch to duck walk, then dropped to her knees and crawled toward the light.

"G'day," a man said.

Ingrid lifted her head and noticed she was back outside. The man who spoke to her held out a hand and helped her to her feet.

"Thanks…" Ingrid paused, trying to remember if she'd gotten his name.

"Noah," the man said.

Ingrid nodded. "Noah. Of course. Thank you."

Ingrid stepped away from the hole and brushed the dirt from her knees. A second later, Geneva's head appeared as she made her way out. Noah helped Geneva to her feet, and she gave him a hug of appreciation.

Geneva let out an extended exhale and sat down with her back to the wall close to the entry. She fished her water bottle from her pack and took a long drink. "How long have we been in there?"

Allie checked her phone. "A little over three hours. Where's Drake?"

Geneva pointed at the hole. "We lost him."

Allie's brow furrowed. "Lost him? How could you lose him? He's not a toddler at a carnival."

"Drake stopped to check something out and told us to keep going," Ingrid said, jumping quickly to Geneva's defense. "He said he'd be right behind us, but when we stopped a couple of minutes later, he was nowhere to be seen."

"We even backtracked to find him," Geneva said. "It's like the cavern opened up and swallowed him whole."

Allie sighed. "What's it like in there?"

Ingrid took a moment to move her hair away from her face. "You know that famous labyrinth in Greek mythology?"

"Yeah."

"Imagine that, but without a Minotaur," Ingrid said.

"Well, to be fair, there might still be a Minotaur in there," Geneva added. "We just didn't see it."

"What did you see?" Allie asked, noticing that Noah had taken a step closer to the threesome and was paying rapt attention.

"Like Ingrid said," Geneva said. "It's just like a labyrinth. Lots of corridors. Some lead to small rooms, then branch out into other corridors. Some of them lead to nowhere and just come to dead ends. It's no wonder people disappear from this place."

"Are you going to go back in there and look for him?" Allie asked.

Geneva shook her head. "I don't think that's a good idea. We might end up getting lost ourselves. It's by pure luck that we got out of there."

"We can't let Drake just be another mysterious disappearance," Allie said.

Geneva stood and embraced Allie. "We're not going anywhere without him. When the others come out, we can come up with a plan to find him."

"What makes you think the others are coming out?" Allie asked. "You were the first ones we've seen leave that hole. Unless there's another exit somewhere, that means there are a whole bunch of people lost in there."

"You think maybe we should call someone for help?" Ingrid asked.

Noah cleared his throat, attracting attention from the three friends. When he saw they were all looking at him. He gestured behind him. "It looks like help has found us."

* * *

Drake sat on the floor, exhausted, and not wanting to walk anymore. He'd trudged through passageway after passageway, wearing himself out in the process. His feet were tender, he had dust in his hair, dirt under his fingernails, and stones in his shoes. He'd stopped twice already to clean out the offending gravel, but they kept crawling in there, as if the rocks were sentient and out to get him.

He pulled the water bottle from his backpack, gave it a

shake, and looked at it. Drake had a half inch of the life-saving liquid left. He considered drinking it and went as far as uncapping the bottle and lifting it to his lips before changing his mind, recapping the bottle, and stowing it in his backpack.

Drake let out a loud moan as he got to his feet, using the wall for support as he did so. Like with every other passageway he'd explored, he found a large rock and placed it right near the entry. That task completed, he turned and stepped into the corridor. Drake didn't know how much distance he'd covered, but he figured it had to be several miles based on all the switchbacks, wide arcs, and back-and-forth dead ends he walked.

Drake carried on for several hundred yards without paying attention to where he was going. When he felt his calves starting to burn, he stopped. He turned and shined the light from where he came and turned around and focused the light ahead.

"Uphill. As if this isn't bad enough, now I have to go uphill," Drake said. His shoulders slumped, and he took a deep breath before resuming his journey.

He put his head down and started counting steps under his breath. Drake had gotten all the way to seven hundred when he perceived a slight change in the slope. When he lifted his head and looked forward, he saw he'd entered a chamber the shape and size of a basketball court. In the center of the room was a large rock, waist high to Drake, and sculpted into a rectangle, and resembling an altar.

Drake moved to the altar and noticed right away engravings on the top. He used the camera on his cell phone to snap several pictures, then inspected the remainder of the altar for others. Finding none, Drake turned his attention to the walls of the room. Only two of the four walls contained engravings, and he was careful to take photos of every inch of them. Then he circled the area again, making sure he hadn't missed a thing.

Drake moved to the corridor, turned around, and took one last picture of the entire space.

"Now all I need to do is find my way out of here," he said, starting down the ramp.

* * *

Allie, Geneva, and Ingrid stood off to the side and waited right where the two rangers told them to.

Both men, who had appeared as if from out of nowhere, dressed in similar outfits composed of khaki pants and short-sleeved khaki button-down shirts with ranger patches on the right sleeve. They were similar in size and stature, with dark skin and black hair. They had similar facial features and could easily pass for father and son.

"Wait here for us to return. Don't follow. Wait here," the older one said as the younger man slipped into the hole without saying a word. Once his partner was clear of the entrance, the older man followed.

"I wonder where they came from," Ingrid said.

"They're from the Arrernte people," Noah said. "This area, along with millions of acres around us, is a part of their ancestral lands. They probably know those caves like the back of their hands. They'll have our friends out here in no time."

"And they're rescue rangers?" Geneva asked.

Noah shook his head. "Not really, but they'll step in when they have to. The rangers are a part of a larger council and are in charge of protecting and caring for the land."

"I'll bet they're not too happy with us wandering around in there," Ingrid said.

Noah nodded. "I suspect you're right. Many of the areas around here are sacred lands to the Arrernte, and it's hard to impress upon visitors to act accordingly."

"Clearly, our event hosts would have known that since they're from this area, right? So why would they bring us to sacred ground?" Allie asked.

Noah shrugged. "You'd have to ask them."

The group heard voices, turned, and saw a head appear from the hole with wavy light-brown hair. Noah leaned down and helped the woman to her feet, and Allie recognized her right away as a member of the team from Germany. Once she was on her feet and away from the hole, the three German men exited. Together, clustered in a small group, they brushed themselves off

"Did you find anything in there?" Allie said. "Any clues to the next location? A set of coordinates or anything?"

The four had a quick conversation in German, then a man broke away from the group and moved to Allie.

"My name is Jonas," he said.

"Allie."

Allie gave the man a once-over. He looked to be in his mid-forties and was broad-shouldered, with short dark brown hair and a weathered but kind-looking face. He shook his head.

"No, we didn't find anything to lead us anywhere," Jonas said with a slight Bavarian accent. "We were lucky the Aborigines came in to find us, or we'd be in there forever."

Allie gave him a soft smile. "I'm glad you made it out of there. Any chance you saw our friend Drake, the man who was with us? He would have been by himself."

Jonas shook his head again, then rejoined his friends.

Twenty minutes after the Germans exited, the Americans and one of the Australian teams exited, with no sign of Drake, any additional coordinates, nor any hint of where to go next among them.

Allie approached Noah, who was standing by himself near the entrance. Every three minutes, he'd crouch and shine a light into the hole before getting to his feet again and pacing in small circles by the opening.

"Are you okay?" Allie asked.

Noah ran his fingers through his hair, then took a step toward the hole before returning to Allie. "I don't understand.

They should be out by now. How long have they been down there?"

Allie checked the clock on her phone. They'd been standing around for a good six hours, but Allie didn't want to say that since she was worried about Drake, too. "I'm sure they'll be back any minute now."

"I hope so," Noah said. He checked the entrance again, then wandered off to talk to the other groups.

Allie looked up into the sky and noticed the sun was on its downward arc in the west, and she began to wonder if they'd make it out of the crater before night fell. She had no desire to climb out of the hole once it turned dark. She was about to talk to Ingrid when she caught someone calling her name, faint, with an echo to it. Allie crouched next to the hole and shined her flashlight into it.

Directly in front of her, Allie spotted the Zoe's long brown hair.

"Hey there," Drake said.

Allie moved her beam past Zoe's torso and spotted Drake's smiling face just above her waist.

"Drake? What's going on?" Allie asked.

"Can you pull her from that side? Be gentle with her. She's unconscious and has a broken leg."

Allie put her hands under the woman's armpits and pulled. Zoe moved toward her a few inches, and Allie moved back. "Noah! Come over here!" Allie called as she repositioned herself and pulled again.

A second later, Noah appeared and moved Allie away.

"Careful with her. She's injured," Allie said.

Noah nodded, then gently pulled Zoe from the entrance. As easy as picking up a bundle of sticks, Noah gathered up the sleeping woman and carried her to even ground and set her down again. Allie's training kicked in and she went to assess the injury, but stopped when she saw it had already been done.

Someone, one of the rangers, she suspected, had splinted the leg using two branches and belts. Allie checked Zoe's pulse and breathing, determined she wasn't in any danger, and turned her attention to Drake, who was in the middle of hugging Geneva.

"Where have you been?" Allie asked.

"Lost, mostly," Drake admitted. "I ran into the Aussies about an hour ago, and the rangers about thirty minutes later."

"What happened to her?" Allie asked, pointing toward Zoe.

"Anyone have any water?" Drake asked. Geneva and Ingrid held up bottles almost in unison. Drake took Geneva's, opened it, and drained most of the refreshing liquid. "Thanks. I didn't catch the entire story, but it sounded like she tripped over something in the dark and fell."

"I'm glad to see you made it out in one piece," Allie said.

"You'll be even gladder when I show you my phone," Drake said as he handed Geneva her empty bottle, took Ingrid's, and began drinking.

CHAPTER THIRTEEN

"We've got to go down there? Seriously?" Ingrid asked, peeling the sunglasses from her face in an attempt to get a better view.

Before them was an expansive, yawning valley carved into the heart of the desert. They stood at the top, and below them, the towering walls appeared layered with shades of ochre, crimson, and streaks of gold. Ingrid spanned for a nice easy trail to take them to the bottom, but all she could see were the jagged striations formed from centuries of wind and water erosion. The valley stretched from twenty feet from where she currently stood, all the way to the horizon, a dramatic contrast to the relatively flat desert plains surrounding it.

Allie let out a protracted sigh. "Yeah."

"How far is it?" Drake asked.

Lenah stepped to the edge of the ridge and peered off in the direction of the rising sun. She adjusted the baseball cap she wore and pointed off in the distance. "Do you see where that ridge breaks off and comes to an end? The one looking like it is pointing to that tree?"

Drake strained his eyes, but he couldn't spot a single feature

Lenah mentioned. "No, actually."

Lenah shrugged, then waved her hand in the air, as if the motion would erase the landscape. "Regardless. That is where we need to go."

"Okay, fine," Drake said. "But I ask again, how far is it?"

"Not far," Lenah said. "I'll have you back in this exact spot within three days, provided you can keep up me."

"I'm sorry," Geneva said. "Did you say three days?"

Lenah nodded. "We told you to prepare for an overnight excursion, didn't we?"

Geneva reared back on her heels, ready to start an argument with the young woman, but Allie stepped in between them and held out her palms to create space.

"Geneva, if you're not up for the trek, that's okay. Ingrid will give you the keys to the Jeep and you can hang out at the hotel for a few days. We'll call you when we need you to pick us up," Allie said.

"No. You won't get any reception here. Well, maybe here, but once we start into the valley you'll be cutoff," Lenah interjected.

"In that case, come back in three days and wait for us," Allie said.

Geneva hesitated for a moment, and her gaze moved from where it locked on Allie, to Ingrid, and finally to Drake. None of their faces showed a glimpse of disappointment, and Drake had a half-crazy smile on his face.

"No, I'm not going back and letting you three go on without me," Geneva said. "I'm just concerned we don't have the supplies needed to make a journey that long."

Lenah stepped around Allie's blockade and placed her hand on Geneva's shoulder. "Whatever we need, the land will provide."

"Well, we should get going then," Drake said, adjusting the straps on his backpack.

Lenah's countenance darkened, and she had a sudden seriousness about her. "Listen to me. We'll go down in a single file line with me in the front and Drake in the back. Do your best to follow the exact path of the person in front of you. If you come across any wildlife, and I mean any, don't engage with it, be it a snake, spider, insect, or common housefly. Also, try not to touch any of the plants once we descend far enough to find them."

"That's it?" Drake said, a touch of sarcasm in his voice.

Lenah passed him a smile. "No, but that's as easy as I can make it for you. Of course, I could have been more direct and reminded you that everything on this continent, be it flora or fauna, is out to kill you."

Drake tipped his head to the side, wiped the grin from his face, and nodded. "Okay. You got me there. Excellent point. I'm sorry."

"Let's go," Lenah said.

Lenah walked back and forth along the ridge, mentally mapping the terrain and looking for the easiest way to the valley floor. Some paths she discounted right away since they involved near-vertical drops, and other potential routes she determined would end up as dead-ends with no way to move forward. After a few minutes, she stopped and pointed at a fifteen-inch gap between two boulders large enough she couldn't see behind.

"Are you sure?" Geneva asked.

Lenah nodded. "The rain runoff goes this way. So will we. Come on."

Without another word, Lenah approached the gap, turned sideways, and slipped through.

"Well, go on," Drake said.

Geneva, closest to the boulders, followed Lenah, with Allie and Ingrid a step behind. Drake, as instructed, brought up the rear.

Drake cleared to the other side of the boulder and almost ran right into Ingrid.

"What's the holdup?" Drake asked.

"Turn this way and look," Ingrid said.

Drake spun ninety degrees and found himself right behind Ingrid's right shoulder. Tall enough to glance over her, he spotted Lenah twenty feet below, descending what looked like steps carved into the side of the valley wall by time and nature. Geneva was only a few steps behind Lenah. Allie had stopped only three stairs from the top. She stood still as a gargoyle on the pinnacle of a Parisian building. Drake noticed Lenah had descended another ten feet, Geneva hot on her heels, both of them unaware movement had stopped above.

Drake put his fingers in his mouth and let out a shrill, extended whistle. "Hey down below!" he yelled.

"Could I have a warning the next time you do that?" Ingrid asked, rubbing the ear that Drake had been close enough to kiss when he whistled.

"Sorry."

Geneva picked up the whistle, stopped, looked back, and recognized the problem right away. She rushed ahead and managed to catch Lenah's arm, preventing her from going any farther.

Drake shifted himself on the narrow ledge so he was hip to hip with Ingrid. "Allie? You okay?"

Allie didn't respond.

"We need to move down to her," Drake said.

Ingrid nodded, and Drake went down two steps and found himself one above Allie.

"Can I come down there? Allie?"

"Yes," Allie whispered.

Drake took the next step and stood next to Allie. He reached out and took her hand.

"I didn't think it would be this scary," Allie said, unprompted. "I thought there might be trees and things to block the view, so I wouldn't have to see what will happen if I fall."

Drake turned his head and took in the view. Below him, he saw Lenah and Geneva waiting for them. A few hundred feet below them, he spotted the brush and trees on the valley floor. Between them and level ground, he saw nothing but open air, and a million places to tumble down the mountain. He'd seen Allie tumble down a mountain once before, and he himself had done so as well, so he understood Allie's apprehension. Going up would be easy, as they would have the next step to guide them. Going down, there was nothing to hold on to, and nothing to prevent them from cartwheeling all the way to the bottom of the gorge.

"Do you want to go back?" Drake asked. "Ingrid is right here. She can take you back to town."

Allie shook her head. "No. I want to go on. My brain says I should go, but right now, my body isn't listening."

"Do you trust me?" Drake asked.

"Of course," Allie said.

"I read this book once where there was a cow stuck on a ledge, but the cow didn't want to move because it got too scared of the view."

Allie chuckled. "Are you comparing me to a cow, Drake?"

"Of course not. But it seems we have the same situation here."

"Did they save the cow?"

"Yes."

"Do I want to know how they did it?"

"No. Just trust me. Ingrid, can you give me that bandanna tied to your backpack?"

Ingrid took the backpack from her shoulders and untied the bandanna attached to the handle and handed it to Drake. Drake unfolded, then refolded it until it was in a three-inch strip.

"Did you make me a blindfold?" Allie asked.

Drake held it out. "Yea."

Allie considered it for a moment, then took the cloth and

secured it over her eyes.

"Can you see anything?" Drake asked, waving his hands in front of Allie's eyes.

"No. Are you sure this is going to work?"

"It did with the cow. And you're almost as smart as a cow. Ingrid will grab onto the strap of your backpack and keep you from tipping over. I'll guide your feet and hopefully catch you if you fall. Should we try a step?"

"Sure," Allie said.

Drake moved down a few steps, so he was even with Allie's feet. He tapped on her right foot. Allie lifted it, and Drake positioned it over the next step.

"Come down," Drake said, guiding Allie's foot as she planted it, then dropped her left foot next to her right.

"Way to go, Allie," Ingrid said in an encouraging tone.

"It's one step. How many more do we have to go?" Allie asked.

Drake turned and looked down. He had no clue how far they'd need to walk like this until they came to an area where Allie seemed comfortable carrying on by herself.

"Well, how about if I keep count, and when we get done, I'll tell you," Drake said.

"That bad, huh?" Allie said.

Drake didn't offer a response.

"I can hear you nodding. Let's get on with it, as quickly as possible, please," Allie said.

For four hours, the group descended the steepest part of the climb from the valley's rim to a section where the steep stairs transitioned into a meandering trail that followed a gentle slope, snaking its way down the side.

Done with the stairs, Ingrid relieved Allie of the blindfold, and they took a fifteen-minute rest for water and to regroup their spirits.

"How much farther from here?" Drake asked.

"Not far," Lenah said. "Maybe a two-hour walk once we get to the valley floor."

"When will that be?" Geneva asked.

Lenah shrugged. "That's hard to say, since there are two options. Option one, we stay on this path, which will probably take a few more hours. Option two, we step off the side here, and it will take no more than ten minutes to get there." Lenah tried to stay serious, but started to laugh, breaking the tension in the air.

"Do you think we'll be down before night falls?" Allie asked. Lenah glanced up at the valley walls where afternoon shadows had begun to grow long. "I hope not. Can you keep up if I go faster?"

"We can try," Allie said.

* * *

"We should have packed air mattresses," Geneva joked as she tried to get comfortable on the hard ground.

"I wouldn't have wanted to haul them down here," Drake said. "Besides, how would we blow them up?"

"That's what we brought you for, Drake," Allie said. "To haul all the luggage."

The women laughed, and Drake did as well. It wasn't the first time he'd heard that.

"Are we going to be safe out here?" Ingrid asked.

Just before the sun had set, Lenah had stopped them on a stretch of level ground, only a hundred feet above the floor. They had descended enough that the air temperature had dropped, and scrub brush and dwarf trees had become common. Lenah had the group scour for usable firewood, while Lenah built a fire ring from rocks, cleared the small patch of debris, and made sure there were no creatures in the immediate area.

"If you stay close to the fire, you should be okay," Lenah said. "If you feel anything crawling or slithering over you in the night, don't move. Just call out for me and I'll come over and take care of it."

"Take care of what?" Drake asked.

"Whatever's trying to eat you, mate," Lenah said.

Drake wanted to ask if she was serious, but he could tell by her expression, even in the dim firelight, that she was.

"We should have packed in some food," Ingrid said.

"No worries," Lenah said, then rose and disappeared from camp.

"That was… interesting," Drake said. "I wonder why Uncle Jarli insisted we bring her along."

"He told me," Allie said.

"He did?"

"Yeah." Allie was sitting cross-legged in front of the fire, and as she mentioned her points, she held up fingers. "First, was because she knows exactly where we need to go and how to get there. Second, to make sure we preserve the sanctity of the site. Third, to make sure you don't die."

"You mean 'we' don't die."

"No, Drake, he mentioned you specifically by name." Allie tried to hold the seriousness of the conversation but laughed at him.

"The laughter is good," Lenah said, coming back from the darkness as if she'd never been away. "It will keep the bigger animals away. Were you expecting company? There are other groups here."

"Where?" Allie said.

Lenah pointed to a spot behind them. "One there, one a few hundred yards in front of us, and one about a quarter-kilo from here."

"How do you know that?" Drake asked.

Instead of an answer, Lenah passed him a look.

"Okay. Can you at least tell us what you're holding there?"

Lenah grinned and held up her catch, an iguana almost as

long as she was tall. "tea, mate."

"That doesn't look like any tea I've ever seen," Ingrid said.

"Nah. You'd know it as dinner."

* * *

Allie knew she was going to die. They'd come to another steep spot on the trail, and Ingrid had given her the blindfold. Once more, she entrusted her friends would help her overcome the tough stretch of terrain, but after only a few feet, someone had pushed her from behind. The blindfold came loose, and Allie saw the ground rapidly rising to meet her.

She screamed.

Allie felt someone grab her shoulders. She opened her eyes and saw Lenah holding her down.

"Calm down. It was just a dream. You almost rolled into the fire."

Allie looked to her side and noticed she was closer to the flames than she ever intended to be.

"You okay now?" Lenah asked.

"Yes, I think so," Allie said.

Lenah released her grip, pushed away from Allie, and stood. "I'll be right back. Don't wake the others if you can help it."

Lenah stepped into the darkness as Allie sat up and glanced around the area. To her right, Ingrid was gently snoring, her back to Allie. The fire had died down some, and through the sporadic flames, he could see Geneva and Drake snuggled together, facing the fire, Drake acting as the big spoon.

Lenah returned shortly, carrying a few items in her fist.

"What do you have there?" Allie asked.

Lenah found a flat stone, and on it she placed a leaf, then something that looked like a piece of bark, and a small white grub. "Just some medicine. Hand me your water bottle."

As Allie reached for her bottle, she watched as Lenah ground the bark and grub together. From her hair, she extracted a sprig of flowers Allie hadn't noticed before. Lenah plucked a few of the tender petals and added them to the paste, added a few drops of water, and used the leaf underneath to shape the paste into a small ball the size of a marble. Lenah unwrapped the leaf and offered it to Allie.

"What am I supposed to do with that?" Allie asked.

"Eat it, of course."

Allie poked it with her finger. It moved a quarter of an inch, then settled back into its original position.

"Come on. It will help with your nightmares. Some say evil spirits haunt this valley," Lenah said, moving her hand closer to Allie. "Look at your friend."

Allie looked through the fire. Drake had started shifting in his sleep, as if pulling away from something. It was a subtle movement, but it was there. Behind her, Ingrid moaned.

"You're sure about this?" Allie said, picking up the unappetizing ball.

"I have thousands of years of tribal history backing me up," Lenah said. "Don't chew. Swallow it down and drink plenty of water afterwards."

Allie took a deep breath, popped the ball into her mouth, and swallowed. It caught in her throat for a moment. She swallowed again, then washed it down with half a bottle of water.

Lenah smiled. "Good. Fifteen minutes and you'll feel better, and your dreams will haunt you no more. I need to go find more grubs. Keep an eye on your friends and make sure they don't fall into the fire."

Before Allie could respond, Lenah stood and left the campsite.

"Did she say we're being haunted?" Ingrid asked.

Allie turned around. Her friend was lying on her side, her head propped up on her hand.

"They forgot to mention that this entire valley is filled with evil spirits that try to kill us in our dreams," Allie said.

"Huh," Ingrid said. "They should have listed that in the brochure."

Allie smiled. "Have a nightmare?"

"Yeah. I got pushed out of a boat and was drowning in the sea. You?"

Allie nodded. "Pushed off a mountain and falling to my death."

"She gave you some medicine to get you to sleep better? Is that what I heard?"

"Yes."

"Think it will help?"

"Well, I don't think it will hurt," Allie said.

"What's in it?"

"Ingrid, you don't want to know. Trust me. Pop it in your mouth, swallow, and don't think about it."

Ingrid shivered. Allie got to her feet, grabbed some wood off the small pile they'd made, and added fuel to the fire. It grew taller and brighter, and Allie moved back to Ingrid and laid down next to her. Ingrid shivered again, so Allie wrapped her arms around her friend.

"Allie?" Ingrid said, sleep returning to her voice.

"Yeah?"

"Did we really eat an iguana for dinner?"

"We did."

Ingrid didn't respond for almost a full minute, and Allie wondered if she had gone back to sleep.

"I wonder what we'll have for breakfast," Ingrid said, just as she nodded off.

CHAPTER FOURTEEN

Allie added more wood to the morning fire to chase the chill from the air while Lenah concentrated on preparing breakfast, which consisted of another, yet decidedly smaller iguana than she served for dinner.

Behind them, Geneva stirred and approached the fire, squatting before it to warm her hands.

"Fun night," she said. "I've never camped in the rough before. I don't suppose there's a fully stocked bathroom around."

Lenah grinned. "You have a variety of trees and bushes from which to pick. Did you pack paper?"

Geneva held up a plastic bag containing toilet tissue and scanned the immediate area for the best place.

"Remember to take a spot before you squat," Lenah advised.

"If you mean make sure there's not something waiting to bite me in the rump while I pee, I'm way ahead of you," Geneva said as she headed for the bush of her choice.

"She's a city girl," Lenah said.

"Yeah, we're all city people," Allie admitted.

"You seem to be a little more adaptable than the others."

"I served in the active military," Allie said.

"They let you serve with a fear of heights?" Lenah asked.

Allie blushed. "I developed that problem after I got out. I had an accident a few years ago that made me a little shy around large hills. That's all."

Lenah nodded. "I understand. I fell from a tree once. Haven't been up one since. You won't have to worry about heights. It's an easy trek to the valley floor, then a straight shot from there to where we're going." Lenah used her fingers to check the iguana, determined it was done, and removed it from the fire completely. "If you want to wake your friends, it's time for brekky."

"How far is it?" Geneva's disembodied voice came from behind the nearby bush.

"Not far, now. Only a three or four-hour walk, depending on how well everyone keeps up," Lenah said.

From behind the bush, Geneva groaned.

* * *

An hour into the hike, Lenah spun around and placed her finger on her lips, the international sign to quiet down. When the four geocachers following her complied, she waved them off of the trail, into the underbrush, and had them crouch low to the ground and put her finger to her lips again.

Two minutes passed. Allie heard a group coming up the trail behind them. She looked back, and saw her friends stayed statue still, as if they'd just taken in Medusa's gaze.

Before the hikers came into view, Allie heard them, all with clear, Midwestern American accents.

"This is getting tedious. You know I hate hiking," Madison said.

"Yeah, what else would you have us do?" Caleb responded.

"You both have access to copters. We should have brought them in," Madison said.

"Hey, wait, stop," Jason said.

Madison and Caleb were about to pass their countrymen hiding in the brush when Jason gave them the order, and they both stopped on a dime and spun to face him.

Allie stared straight through the bush and saw the Spanish galleon on Caleb's belt buckle in front of her.

Jason stepped up to the two until his face was within only inches of both of theirs.

"You two need to slip back into character. We're here as geocachers trying to win a prize, remember? So, no. We're not bringing in helicopters. We're not bringing in any outside help at all. If you've got a problem with the hike, you go back, and we'll cut you out of the commission. Is that what you'd prefer?" Madison swayed, as if she wanted to step backward, but she stayed in place. "No, Sir."

"Or would you prefer to have an accident out here? It's not like we haven't arranged them before."

Madison hesitated.

"Well?"

"No, Sir," she answered.

"You both need to remember that I'm in charge, and I call the shots on this mission. When we get paid, you can both go back to your regular lives and will never need to take another order from me. Until the money hits the bank, you will do exactly as I say. So turn around, and hike."

As ordered, Madison and Caleb spun without a word and continued down the trail with Jason right behind them.

Allie and her friends stayed in position. Four minutes later, Lenah gave the okay, and they all climbed back onto the main trail.

"What do you make of that?" Drake asked.

"I don't think they're who they say they are," Allie said. "Ingrid and I did research on all the other teams in this competition, and it seemed suspicious at the time that a team with their geocaching stats got chosen for an event like this, and I'm guessing that's the case. Sounds like they are here as ringers."

"What should we do?" Geneva asked.

Allie shrugged. "There's nothing to do at this point except keep an eye on them. We still have as good of a chance of finding the prize as everyone else."

"Is there anyone else we should watch?" Drake asked.

"Yeah. The other Australian team," Allie said.

"Not the Germans?" Geneva said. "In the movies it's always the Germans."

Allie smiled. "Not this time. At least we don't think so. Lenah, let's get going. I don't want to get there too far behind them."

For the next two hours, the trail followed the valley floor, and the group marched in relative silence, with Lenah on the point, keeping them as close to the other team as they could, but as neither Geneva nor Ingrid were used to extended hikes, they needed to stop and rest more often along the way.

At the beginning of their fourth hour on the trail, it seemingly dead-ended at a thick cluster of boab trees, and Lenah stopped.

"From here, you'll need to go on your own. My ancestors are here, and I'm not prepared to honor them in the proper way."

"What if we need you?" Geneva asked.

"It's not far, and the sound carries in this place, so if you need me, call and I'll come. Otherwise, I'll wait for you here," Lenah answered. Being her last words, she selected a spot in the shade, sat, and extracted a paperback from her backpack.

Allie nodded. "Okay. All we need to do is find a way through these trees?"

"Step forward and keep moving. The way the trunks align creates an optical illusion," Lenah said without looking up from the page.

Allie took a step and reached out for the trunk of the tree on her right. Her palm against the bark, she reached for the tree on the left, lost her balance, and lurched forward, touching the tree only after she'd stumbled three feet farther than she'd expected to. Her hand came into contact with the trunk, slid off, and before she knew it, she was on her knees.

"Allie?" Drake called.

"I fell."

Allie detected footsteps, and a couple of seconds later, Drake helped her to her feet. Geneva and Ingrid stood right behind him.

"It's like a maze of funhouse mirrors," Drake said. "I'll take the lead if you want."

Allie brushed off her knees while Drake stepped in front and held his hand back. The team got the idea, and they moved as one unit, hand-in-hand, until they broke through the trees and found themselves in a large circular area surrounded by boab trees.

"How are we going to find our way out of here? Everything looks the same," Drake said.

"I got this," Ingrid said. She stopped, removed the bandanna from her backpack, and tied it to a low branch where they'd stepped from the trees.

"Good job, you," Drake said. "Now, I guess we need to join the hunt to see what we can find."

"We don't know what we're looking for," Ingrid said.

"True, but neither to they," Drake said, pointing toward the center of the circle where the Americans and the Germans were involved in a conversation. As they observed the group, the Australian team broke through the trees on the far side and headed directly for the others. "Let's go."

As one, the group stepped into the circle and started walking toward the larger group. Around them were indents in the ground, each six feet long and three feet wide.

"Wait. Hold on," Geneva said. "Are we in a burial ground?"

The group stopped and looked around. There were no traditional markers, as seen in the cemeteries they were used to, but several of the indents contained evidence that items placed on them, from withered flowers and fruit to small cairns.

"I think so," Drake said.

"Then uh-uh. I'm not going," Geneva said, turning to return to the tree line.

Drake followed and grabbed her by the elbow before she got too far. "What's going on?"

"In the dream I had last night, we were here. In this place, and something bad happened to one of us. We're not going to find anything among those graves except death. That's what the voice said."

Drake let go of her elbow and put his hands on both of her shoulders. "Come on, Gen. That was only a bad dream. We all had them. But dreams can't hurt us."

Geneva shook her head. "No. It was a premonition. Not a dream. I'm not going in there." She pulled away from Drake and retreated to the trees.

"All right," Drake said. "Stay where we can see you, okay?"

Geneva nodded, and Drake moved back to Allie and Ingrid. When he reached them, the three walked toward the larger group.

"Howdy," Allie said when they'd gotten to within a few feet.

"So, the gang's all here," Caleb said.

"What's the plan? More collaboration, or are we striking out on our own this time?" Allie asked, moving right in front of Caleb. Although she stood a few inches shorter than him, she gave no indication that he threatened her in any way.

"There's nowhere to hide out here. When someone finds something, everyone else is going to know about it right away anyway, so I think we're all better off on our own," Caleb said.

"Works for us," Allie agreed.

"Good. Then why don't you take that area over there," Caleb started, pointing off in the distance.

"Hold on there, mate," Jack said, his tone sounding

unfriendly, despite the Australian accent. "You're not in charge here, so you're not assigning areas. We're all free to wander about where ever we like."

Caleb put his hands up in surrender. "Okay, okay. You win. Everyone goes where they want to go. Come on." Caleb left the group, Madison and Jason trailing behind him.

The other three teams waited for a moment before heading off in their own directions. Drake, Allie, and Ingrid hung back the longest, and once they saw the other three groups select destinations at random, Drake pointed off to the northwest, where no other team had ventured and started walking.

"Do you have any idea about what we're looking for, Allie?" Drake asked.

Allie shook her head. "We haven't seen actual coordinates in this game for some time, so I would expect we're looking for more symbols."

"Why the change?" Drake asked.

"That's obvious, isn't it?" Ingrid said.

Ingrid had been trailing behind the other two, and when she spoke, Drake and Allie stopped and turned to face her.

"Tell me," Drake said.

Ingrid looked at Allie, and Allie nodded.

Ingrid looked around to make sure no one else was nearby, took a step toward her friends, and dropped her voice to a whisper. "We're not competing to win some fancy geocaching contest. We're out here searching for the stone of the Rainbow Serpent."

Drake grinned, saw the stoic looks facing him, and became serious. "You're not kidding."

Ingrid shook her head. "I'm guessing this whole competition was a ruse to get us here. An invitation-only event where the world's best geocachers are competing, yet there are two teams with barely a thousand finds between them? I'm betting that the event hosts tried to find the stone, couldn't, and came up with this elaborate idea to search it out."

Drake considered the point for a moment. "What do you think?"

Allie gathered her thoughts for a second. "That would explain why there are literal treasure hunters out here."

"So what do we do?" Drake asked.

"If Uncle Jarli's stories have any truth to them at all, there's no way we should let anyone besides us get to that stone."

Drake nodded. "We'd better get to it."

* * *

Geneva watched from the safety of the trees while her friends approached the larger group, then followed as everyone broke off and went their own way. She took a deep breath, intending to traipse across the field and join her friends. She took a single step toward them and a chill started on her spine right at the base of her coccyx and traveled right up to her temple. Geneva shuddered, then retreated to the safety of the trees.

Undaunted, Geneva eyed her friends as they searched the ground, moving ever closer to the trees opposite her. An idea came to her, and Geneva started to walk, staying close to the trees as she made her way around the perimeter of the circle. Once she stepped into the circle when she encountered a tree that had overgrown the boundary. The ice against her spine returned, and she rushed around the tree until she shook the feeling. By the time she made her way to the other side, her friends had almost reached the perimeter.

"How's it going?" Geneva asked.

Drake, so focused on the ground, hadn't noticed her approach, and seemed shocked when he heard her speaking. He looked up and smiled. "Hey, there."

Drake went to Geneva, took her into a hug, and gave her a quick kiss. "Did you change your mind?"

"No. I tried. But every time I cross some invisible barrier, I get a feeling of dread I can't shake. Something bad is going to happen here, Drake. Can we leave? Please?"

Drake looked into Geneva's eyes and saw a genuine look of concern there. "I wish we could, but Allie and Ingrid think there's more going on here than we signed up for. We need to see this thing through, I think. Do you understand?"

Geneva nodded. "Not really."

Drake smiled again. "Can you hold on for a little while?"

Geneva nodded again. "You three be careful out there."

Drake scowled. "That won't be hard. There's nothing out here to find, unless they buried the secret with the other poor souls around here."

Geneva stared at him for a moment. "No, I don't think that's the case at all. I think we'll find what we need somewhere around here."

"Okay. We'll get back to it. I don't want to be around here anymore than we need to be," Drake said. He gave Geneva another kiss and left her in the trees and rejoined Allie and Ingrid, who were crisscrossing the area, heads down, searching the ground for anything out of the ordinary.

Geneva watched them for a while, then something screeched to her left. At first it sounded like a wailing baby, but the initial cry broke off, extended, raised in pitch and volume, then stopped and repeated. She listened to it a second time. The leaves ahead of her rustled and she saw the outline of an enormous bird walking through the trees.

A large white head on an extended neck appeared directly before her, spotted Geneva, then pulled away and headed in the opposite direction. Intrigued by the large beast, Geneva waited a second and silently stepped into the trees in an attempt to follow it. She stepped deeper into the underbrush, shuffled around a boab tree, and came into a small clearing.

The bird, looking more like its dinosaur cousin, picked

through the fallen leaves looking for food. It seemed aware that Geneva was nearby, but didn't seem to care. Geneva watched the bird for a while, and when it grew bored and walked off, Geneva noticed for the first time a large boulder. It was taller than her by three feet, and since it looked like an egg standing on end, she assumed it wasn't a natural occurrence. She moved to it and placed her flattened palm against it, expecting crags and bumps.

"Smooth," she said, rubbing the stone and trying to find a spot where it didn't feel like polished granite beneath her fingertips.

Geneva kept her hand on the stone and moved around to the other side. The sight of writing chiseled into the stone surprised her, and beneath the words were several symbols. She removed her phone from her pocket, took several pictures and walked around the monument two more times to ensure she hadn't missed anything. When she determined she hadn't, she checked the reception, saw she had zero bars, then picked her way back to the circle.

Coming out of the trees, she noticed Drake, Allie, and Ingrid were almost in the circle's center. The German and Australian groups were headed in her direction, and the Americans seemed excited about a location fifty yards to her right.

Geneva stood at the edge of the trees, waving her arms in front of her, trying to attract her friends' attentions, but when she didn't, she began to jog along the tree line to a spot where she'd be in one of their direct sight lines.

Ingrid spotted Geneva first and jogged to her friend.

"I got it. We can go," Geneva said.

"What?"

Geneva turned around so her back faced the circle and showed the pictures to Ingrid.

"Yeah, you got something there," Ingrid said. "I'll go get the others."

Ingrid glanced across the field to find Drake and Allie, and the second she spotted them, she heard two people scream. Drake and Allie stood for a second like deer frozen before an oncoming car, then took off running across the field toward the American team.

"Go get Lenah," Ingrid screamed to Geneva, then ran to catch up with her friends.

Ingrid covered the distance quickly, then stopped when Allie turned around and put out her hands.

"Don't come over here. Go back," Allie ordered.

Without question or comment, Ingrid took a few steps backward, then stopped.

"What's going on?" Ingrid asked.

"They fell into a snake den," Allie said.

"What kind of snakes?" Ingrid asked.

Allie took a slow step, then looking into the open grave two people had fallen into. "Big ones. With teeth."

"Help me," Caleb pleaded. He'd fallen into the pit first, with Jason right on top of him. Madison had somehow avoided the pit, but was rolling on the ground, writhing in pain and grabbing her left knee.

"Calm down, and keep quiet," Allie said. She took another step closer to the pit and looked down. "Are those pythons?" she asked Drake.

"How would I know? I'm not an herbalist," Drake said, leaning in and looking at the half dozen brown snakes that had taken offense to having their den disrupted.

"I think you mean herpetologist, not herbalist," Allie said. She crouched to get a closer look. "I'm pretty sure these are pythons. Can you find me a sturdy stick or two, about four feet long?"

Drake nodded, then took off toward the trees to search for the item.

While Drake was away, Allie turned her attention to Madison.

"Are you okay?" Allie asked.

Madison didn't answer, so Allie had Ingrid hold her down while Allie tore away Madison's pant leg to get a better look at the knee.

"The bad news is, I think you blew your knee out. The good news is you won't have to worry about any long hikes in the immediate future. Ingrid, stay with her, and make sure she doesn't move."

When Allie returned to the pit, Drake had returned with three long branches. She selected one, then offered another to Drake. "Let's pull out the snakes. Carefully. Set them off to the side, and they should slither away. Then we can get the guys out of there."

With Drake following Allie's lead, they fished whatever snakes from the pit they could find, then placed them on the ground and watched as they moved on. Once clear of serpents, Drake hoisted Jason from the pit, who suffered nothing more than a bruised elbow. Caleb fared much worse, with two broken legs, which Allie triaged.

"Looks like you didn't need me after all," Lenah said.

Allie shrugged. "If you could arrange a ride back, that would be cool."

CHAPTER FIFTEEN

"Lenah told me how you saved those people. I'm impressed," Uncle Jarli said as he welcomed the group into his building.

Allie shrugged off the comment. "It was nothing. I was a medic in the military, so my training kicked in. When I see someone needing medical attention, I go into an automated response mode."

Uncle Jarli shook his head. "Perhaps. I was more impressed with the way you handled the snakes. It appears you gave the animals as much respect as the humans."

Allie waved that off, too. "They were innocents. It's not like they wanted people to come and disturb their sanctuary."

Uncle Jarli smiled, then laughed. "I think you might carry some of the spirit of my ancestors in you."

Allie nodded, then got down to business. "We have more photographs we'd like you to take a gander at."

Without waiting for a response, Geneva stepped up and handed her phone to Uncle Jarli. As he moved from image to image, his bright smile faded and his face tightened, like he'd just sucked on a lemon.

"No. There's nothing here." Uncle Jarli tossed the phone in Geneva's direction. She reached out to grab it, but batted it farther into the air, and it was only a last second catch from Drake that prevented it from hitting the floor.

"Hey," Geneva protested.

"I'm sorry. I need to go now. There's another appointment I need to get to," Uncle Jarli said as he began ushering the group out the door that he'd just welcomed them through. Ingrid, having not made it fully in the building before the reversal happened, backed up almost into the street to avoid the hasty exit of her friends.

"Uncle Jarli, please…" Allie started.

Uncle Jarli waved at her, and continued to walk forward, using his bulk to push them toward the door. Once Allie got both feet on the concrete sidewalk, the door closed behind her.

Drake turned around in exasperation. "What just happened?"

Allie shook her head. "I'm not sure."

"What did you show him?"

Allie glanced to her left and spotted Lenah back on her favorite bench, still pouring through a paperback. "Pictures from the burial ground yesterday. They seemed to upset him and he kicked us out."

"Mind if I take a look?" Lenah asked, putting her book upside-down on the seat so she wouldn't lose her page.

Geneva handed Lenah her phone, and Lenah took her time to study the images. "Where did you find these? And how?"

"They were outside of the burial ground area. On a large rock, just inside the trees," Geneva said.

"The rock, tell me about it. Was it a big one? Smooth?"

Geneva nodded. "It reminded me of a chicken egg sitting upright."

Lenah handed the phone back and shook her head. "It can't be. It's all a myth. Stories to entertain the children."

"What's the story?" Allie asked. "Clearly, those markings aren't a myth. We've got pictures of them. Come on. Help us out here."

Lenah sat silent for almost a full minute, then nodded. "The ancestors tell the story about how the serpent's stone will show itself once in the spirit realm and twice in the water realm before revealing itself to whoever it deems worthy of finding it."

Geneva grabbed her phone and moved to a picture that showed the stone in its entirety, with the engraved name clearly in the frame. "I thought that this was a monument to a person. Is that not the case?"

"No. This is a monument to the Rainbow Serpent."

"And the symbols?" Allie asked.

"They reference the dry valley."

"Dry valley? What's that?" Drake asked.

"It's not a valley in the traditional sense. Nothing like we visited yesterday. It's more of a large fissure, I guess you'd say. Not a large one, either. It's maybe a half kilometer wide by a kilometer long. From the air, it looks like a stab wound in the earth," Lenah said.

"Can we go in there?" Drake asked.

Lenah nodded. "Yes. It's not as hard as you'd think. There's a trail on the southern tip that slopes right in. The fissure is only a hundred meters deep at most."

"Have you been there?" Allie asked.

"Yes, I've—"

"Lenah. Come here, child," Uncle Jarli growled. As they were talking, no one had seen him open the door.

Without a word, Lenah got up from the bench and entered the building, leaving her book behind. Uncle Jarli slammed the door behind them.

"Well, now what?" Drake asked.

"Now we need to find out where this valley is," Allie said.

"I have an idea where we can do that," Ingrid said.

"Where?"

Ingrid pointed across the street. Up the block, she saw the town's public library. "I'll bet they have a map in there. Or at the least, someone who can give us an idea of where to go."

The four friends walked to the corner, crossed the street, and headed into the freestanding building that served as the library. It stood two stories high, had a brick facade, and a large, four-faced clock on top with both hands stuck permanently on twelve.

The large door creaked as Drake pulled it open, and they stepped into the library. In front of them was an unmanned desk, and beyond that were the stacks.

"Where do we go?" Drake asked.

"Local history? Maybe there's a cartography section somewhere," Allie said. "Everyone spread out and look around."

Drake, Allie, and Geneva headed off to different corners of the library to search for documentation. Ingrid spotted a sign for the ladies' room and headed there. On her way back, she noticed an elderly man with long, white hair sitting in a rocking chair and reading a newspaper.

"Hello," Ingrid said out of habit.

"G'day," the man responded. "What are you searching for?"

Ingrid had almost passed the man, but she stopped and turned around to face him. "Pardon me?"

"You and them. What are you looking for?" the man repeated. "I don't usually have visitors in here. Especially at this time of the year. A few people a day at best, and certainly not strangers to our town. What are you looking for?"

Ingrid stammered. "Just information. A valley. A rift, a fissure. I don't know what I would call it."

"The anomaly is what you should call it. It's a tear right there in the middle of the desert, like a giant troll slammed an ax into it."

"I guess you know it?" Ingrid said.

"Know it? I own it. It's on my land," the old timer said.

"Can you take us to it?"

The man stared at Ingrid for a while as he smacked his lips while trying to decide.

"All right. Let's go."

Ingrid rounded up her friends and met the man outside of the library, where he waited in a faded red 1964 Ford pickup truck. Although the man offered to give them a ride, he waited while the group retrieved their Jeep from up the block, then followed him out of town.

They rode in silence for fifteen minutes on the paved highway, Ingrid doing her best to keep up with the man who drove way over the posted speed limit. Ingrid feathered the brakes when the pickup slowed, then turned onto a dirt road made of nothing fancier than tire tracks. The truck sped up, and once again, Ingrid did her best to follow while her passengers were jostled inside the Jeep, trying hard to stay seated.

Twenty minutes later, the man stopped his truck on a dime, causing a cloud of dust to float in the air, and Ingrid pulled in right beside him. Twenty yards ahead of them were two vehicles, parked in a V, nose to nose in front of a cattle gate.

"I had to fence this entire thing with all the trespassers that would come in here," the man said, pointing to the barbed wire fence that started on one side of the gate and presumably looped around the entire valley. "I didn't mind at first, but when the territory told me that I would be liable if anyone got hurt here, I closed it right up. Can you imagine? Me liable for someone else's trespass. Now it looks like I need to go down there and shoo another bunch of people off my land."

The man leaned into the pickup and extracted a rifle from the gun rack. He made a move to the gate, and Ingrid stepped in front of him.

"Hold on," Ingrid said, putting her hand on his arm. "There's a chance we know who these people are. I understand you don't want random strangers invading your property, so why don't you let us go down and bring them up?"

"You'd do that for old Hap?"

Ingrid smiled. "Sure. Put your gun back in your truck, and we'll be back with them in no time."

Hap scratched his chin where a rough beard was coming in. "All right. Go." Hap dug a key out of his pocket, unlocked the chain around the gate, and swung it open so Ingrid and her friends could pass. "Oh. Be mindful down there. If you feel any tremors, you get back up here, quickly."

Drake stopped. "What do you mean by tremors?"

Hap looped the chain over the fence post and put the open lock inside a link. "Like an earthquake. I've had geologists down there studying it. Some say it's the result of mining operations from a hundred years ago, some say it's a natural gas pocket. One fella claimed I'm right on top of a fault line, which was never proven. Regardless, if the ground starts shaking under your boots, you get out."

The group passed through the gate and hiked straight ahead for thirty yards where they came to a set of eight crumbling concrete stairs that took them from ground level down to the start of what looked to be the remnants of a dirt ramp leading to the valley floor. Where they started looked like the tip of a spear, with the walls only eight feet from each other, but as they descended, the walls widened, and once they got to the bottom, they ended up more or less in the valley's center.

"Looks like a football," Drake said as he observed the surrounding space. "Do we know where to go? Or even what to look for?"

"I've been thinking about that," Allie said. "Lenah mentioned signs in the spirit world, and in the water world. If the burial ground represented the spirit world, then I would guess we need to find something in here having to do with water."

Allie glanced around at the valley floor. There was no vegetation of any kind, nor any water source that she could see from where they stood. The landscape was ripe with large boulders, dead trees, sand mounds, and piles of debris everywhere that had blown into the hole over the years. It reminded her of a garbage dump.

"Let's get on with it. This place gives me the creeps," Allie said.

Drake took the lead, and the rest followed behind him in line, tracing his steps as he navigated around obstacles as they plodded toward the opposite side of the valley. Drake climbed to the top of a four-foot-high berm.

"Holy cow, would you look at that?" he said.

"What?" Geneva asked.

Geneva was still on the downhill, so Drake reached out, took her hand, and pulled her up. After Geneva found her footing, Drake aided Allie and Ingrid as well, and as one, they stared ahead at the large, petrified tree directly in front of them.

"I've never seen such a thing," Allie said as she stepped down from the berm and headed to the monument. As she walked, she looked up, taking in the breadth and width of it. The massive tree stood thirty feet tall, with a trunk seven feet wide, and unlike most petrified trees she'd ever seen, had thick branches extending out from the trunk. Several had surrendered their own weight to gravity over time, but there were still an impressive amount of them attached to the tree.

"Do you think we'll find the symbols here? It looks like this tree has been around forever," Geneva said.

As they walked around the perimeter of the tree, they found the German team on the other side, examining the trunk.

Anna, crouching before the trunk, jumped up and rushed to Allie, who was in front of the others by a foot.

"*Nein,*" Anna said, holding up her hand to prevent Allie from moving any closer.

"What?" Allie asked.

"We are looking here," Anna said. Her green eyes, which

had a warm glow to them the last time Allie had spoken to her, now appeared cold and harsh. "You can search elsewhere."

"And you shouldn't be here," Ingrid said, stepping beside Allie. "You're trespassing. The property owner wants you out."

Anna rolled her eyes and waved a hand. "We will go when we're ready to go."

Ingrid wanted to say something else, but Allie grabbed her by the arm and pulled her away. "Not worth it. Let's go."

The group hiked on for fifty yards before anyone spoke.

"Do you think they found something there?" Geneva asked.

"Possibly. They seemed awfully interested in that tree," Drake said. "On the way back, we'll check it out and see if there's anything of note."

As they walked on, the group made small talk, and they'd almost made it to the far side of the valley when they looked off to their left and spotted one man from the Australian geocaching team carrying a rock the size of a basketball from out of a small cave in the sheer valley wall. He dumped the rock on a small pile of debris, wiped his brow, and disappeared back into the cave.

"Should we go see what's going on over there?" Geneva asked.

Allie shook her head. "No way. I've had enough of caves for one trip. For all trips, actually."

"I told Hap I would tell them to come up," Ingrid said. "I could go do that and find out what they're up to."

Geneva nodded. "Let's go."

"What if something happens to you?" Allie asked.

"Like what? You'll be here standing guard to save us if you see any shenanigans, right?"

"I can be," Drake said.

Geneva laughed. "Not you. Allie. Allie can stand guard."

Geneva grabbed Ingrid by the arm and they headed off in the cave's direction, with Allie and Drake watching them.

"You think they'll be okay?" Drake asked.

"Yep."

"There's not much to see here. The valley tapers in to another point about a hundred yards from here."

Allie looked at Drake. "Why don't you go check it out, and I'll keep an eye on the girls."

Drake nodded. He hesitated for a second and then continued on his way, paying more attention to his footing than to the sights in front of him. Before long, he realized he'd come to the end of the valley and stopped in front of a vertical wall. He looked up, saw a ledge far above him, took a few backward steps, tripped over a branch, and fell flat on his backside, knocking the breath out of him.

As he rolled onto his right hip to get into a position to stand, he looked down and in the stone he saw the faint outline of three fish, preserved as fossils in the rock. Quickly, Drake clambered to his feet and studied the ground around the area, finding more fossils as he did. Before long, he realized that he now stood in the remains of an ancient pool created by a waterfall.

Drake looked up again and realized at once what he thought was a ledge was actually a lip from which flowed a long-gone river. He stepped back to the wall he'd almost run into and ran his hands on it, brushing away the accumulated dirt, dust, and debris of several decades.

At last, he uncovered an arc chiseled into the stone, and he searched around until he found a stick and a small rock to use to clear away the rest of the symbol. Once done with the first, he easily found four more and went to work uncovering them. Within twenty minutes, he stepped back, satisfied that he'd found everything he was going to, retrieved his phone, and snapped several pictures.

Saddened there was nothing he could do to hide his find, Drake turned and headed back to his friends.

"Where have you been?" Allie asked when Drake finally caught up to them.

Drake pulled out his phone and showed them the pictures. "I think I have what we came here to find. Did you have any luck with the Australians over there?"

Ingrid frowned. "They told me to bugger off. Except they used terms I didn't understand, and they didn't sound quite so friendly."

Allie nodded. "It seems all the camaraderie has finally worn off, and it's every team for themselves."

"Good," Drake said. "Then I won't feel bad about not sharing what I got."

The ground lurched. Ingrid took a step backward to keep her balance, stepped on Geneva's foot, and toppled to the ground. The mini-quake lasted for several seconds, and when it finished, the four friends looked at each other, waiting for something else to happen.

"What the hell was that?" Drake asked. He put out a hand to help Ingrid to her feet, a gesture she accepted.

"That was our invitation to get the hell out of here," Allie said. "Can you run, Ingrid?"

Ingrid nodded. "Try to keep up with me."

CHAPTER SIXTEEN

Before anyone could move, the ground moved again, violently enough to cause the four of them to drop to their knees. From within the earth, a large groan erupted, as if the desert was calling out in agony. They stayed close to the ground and waited for the rumble to stop, and after thirty seconds, got back to their feet.

"Anyone else catch that?" Geneva asked.

Allie nodded. "Sounded like a scream."

Drake pointed to the far wall. "It looks like the Australians are in trouble."

Drake rushed to the cave, mindful of his footing, while Allie, Geneva, and Ingrid followed close behind. When they got to within a few feet, they encountered a pile of rubble where the cave entrance had been. From inside, they heard a cry for help.

Allie stepped as close as she could. "Hey in there! Can you hear me?"

There was a momentary pause. "Is there someone out there?"

"We'll get you out. Hold on!" Drake yelled as he stepped forward. "Stand back."

Allie, Geneva, and Ingrid moved away from the rockslide and Drake stood to the side and began to push any loose rocks and stones away from the cave opening. As the debris settled, the women moved the larger stones away from the entrance.

"Hey," Drake said, peering into a small hole he'd uncovered. Enough light made its way inside to spot a tall and lean man with long, dirty blond hair leaning against the wall. "Jack? That's your name, isn't it? Jack?"

The man didn't move or make any sign he'd overheard Drake speak.

"Allie? Can you give it a try?" Drake asked, stepping away from the wall.

Allie took Drake's place and looked into the hole. "That is you, isn't it, Jack? Can you answer me?"

Jack snapped out of his trance and rushed toward the hole. His eyes were wide, drenched in sweat, and he twitched in a way that made him appear to be on drugs. "You need to get us out of here! There's no air! We're going to die in here!"

"Shh," Allie said. "Jack, look at me."

He lifted his head, and the two made eye contact.

"I think you're having a panic attack," Allie whispered. "Can you close your eyes and take some deep breaths for me?"

Jack shook his head. "There's no air! We're going to suffocate!"

"Jack. Eyes on me. You can see me, right?"

Jack gave her a furtive glance and timidly nodded.

"I'm outside, Jack. In the air, and all that air is coming into you. Please. Close your eyes and breathe with me. Inhale and exhale as I tell you to, okay? I know you can do it."

Jack nodded again and closed his eyes. For a few minutes, Allie led him through breathing exercises until his body language showed he was no longer in fight-or-flight mode.

"Open your eyes," Allie said.

Jack did.

"Hi there," she said. "Doing better?"

"Yes."

"Where are your friends? Are any of you hurt?"

Jack held up his right arm. "I might have sprained my wrist. The others are back in the cave. I can't get to them."

"Okay," Allie said. "We're going to get you out of there and come back for your friends. Stand as far back as you can and let us do all the work."

Jack nodded and retreated as far as he could into the cave, which was only about five feet. Allie watched him, then turned back to her friends.

"We need to bust them all out of there. He hurt his wrist, so he won't be able to help."

Drake and Allie swapped places again, and Drake spent a few minutes checking over each of the piled boulders. Starting at the top of the pile, he attempted to pull rocks away, and although he removed a handful from the stack, the majority stuck tight.

"I think we're going to need a lever or two to clear this away," Drake said, stepping away from the entrance.

"We're on it," Ingrid said, pulling Geneva with her on a quest to find something to use.

"I'd better go, too," Drake said. "Stay here in case he needs anything. We'll be right back."

Allie cleared away the rocks Drake had fallen, then returned to the hole. "We'll have you out in a few minutes, Jack. Sit tight."

Drake returned first with a six-foot piece branch bleached white by time and sunlight. He moved to the rock pile and turned his attention to the highest rock he could reach. He jammed the branch behind the toaster-oven-sized rock and pushed with all his might. The rock moved an inch, raining dirt to the ground, then gave way and tumbled to the earth. It hit the boulder on the bottom of the pile and rolled forward, stopping an inch in front of Allie's left foot.

"Now we're making progress," Drake said as he selected the

next boulder to work on, this one the size of a beach ball. He wedged the branch behind the rock, then threw his entire body weight into the lever. Once again, dirt fell to the earth, but the boulder didn't budge. Drake repositioned the branch and his body, then tried again. This time, there was a loud groan, then the branch snapped in two. The piece he held snapped back and hit him in the head, and Drake lost his balance, staggered backward, tripped on a rock and fell onto his back.

Allie was at his side in an instant and didn't let him move until she gave him a quick check to make sure he had broken nothing.

"So much for progress," Allie said. "Sit up."

Drake did as he was told while Allie removed her pack. From inside, she extracted a handful of fast-food napkins and pressed them against Drake's temple.

"Hold these in place. You're bleeding."

Drake placed his hand on the napkins and applied pressure.

"How does it feel?" Allie asked. "You conked your head pretty good there."

"I think I'll have a killer headache later," Drake said. He pulled the napkins from his head, then sensed the blood drip down his forehead and wiped it away with the napkin. "This isn't working."

"You need to keep pressure on it," Allie said, moving his hand to the wound. "Press."

Allie noticed someone approaching, turned back, and spotted Geneva and Allie returning. They each had items over their shoulders like soldiers on a march.

Geneva spotted Drake lying on the ground, dropped the branch she carried, and ran to his side.

"What happened?" she asked, kneeling beside him.

"Branch broke and hit me in the head. I'm fine," Drake said.

"Let me see," Geneva ordered, a stern expression on her face.

"Later," Allie said. "He's still bleeding."

Geneva was about to argue the point when there was a loud rumble that rolled through the valley. Since there was a bright blue sky above them, they knew it wasn't thunder, and instead came from below and not above.

"Forget Drake. We need to get those men out of the cave and get out of this hole," Allie said. "What did you find?"

Geneva retrieved the length of branch she had found. Ingrid showed off the iron bar that looked to be a remnant from a fence post.

Drake made a move to stand, but Allie put a hand on his shoulder. "You can get up, but you need to move out of the way, and that's it. If you get dizzy or have double vision, let me know right away."

Drake wanted to object, but Allie helped him to his feet and led him a safe distance from the cave. Once she got him situated, she joined Ingrid and Geneva, who had taken up positions on either side of the entrance and were arguing about which boulders to go after. Allie held up the progress while she took a look at the rockslide. Rather than attack the whole thing, she pointed out only four large rocks she wanted cleared, then put Geneva and Ingrid to work to carry out her plan.

Working together, the women dislodged all four boulders in short order, and the rest toppled like dominoes. Allie entered the cave first and escorted Jack over to where Drake had found a spot to sit down. Once she gave Jack a once over and determined he'd only suffered a slight wrist sprain, Allie entered the cave, despite her desire to stay outside.

Although the entrance to the cave was only shoulder-wide, the passageway widened as it snaked fifteen feet into the side of the valley. There, the women came to another spot where the ceiling had collapsed. When Allie got inside, Ingrid and Geneva were already at work, clearing away whatever they could carry.

Once they'd moved whatever they were able by hand, Allie stepped in and analyzed what she felt needed to come down, and

Geneva and Ingrid muscled their way through whatever Allie needed them to. After fifteen minutes of steady, sweaty work, a few rocks rolled from near the ceiling, and a moment later, an arm came through the hole, followed by a head with dark, messy hair, and a well-groomed beard.

When he discovered the women, he smiled. "Lachlan, you'll never believe it. Sheilas have rescued us!"

Another rumble came up through the ground. Inside the cave, the groan reverberated off of the walls.

"We need to get out of here. Now," Allie said.

Ingrid and Geneva rushed from the room, and Allie stayed behind long enough to make sure that Ethan would make his way through the hole. Once his shoulders came into view, Allie left the cave and waited for the men outside.

After three minutes Ethan and Lachlan rushed from the cave. A moment later, the ground shook again and everyone watched as an enormous chunk of the valley wall broke free and buried the cave entrance completely.

"I guess we owe you sheilas a coldie," Ethan said as he watched the dust settle.

"I assume that's a beer," Geneva said. "We'll take it once we're all back up top."

The earth rumbled again. The three Australian men didn't say a word among them, but as one, they started to race away as fast as their legs would take them.

"Well, that was rude. They didn't even say goodbye," Ingrid said.

"Let's take that up with them later," Allie said. "Drake, let me check your head."

Drake removed the napkins, and Allie checked the wound. The blood had eased, but not stopped.

"You think you can walk fast?" Allie asked.

The ground rumbled again.

Drake stood. "You bet. Let's get the hell out of here."

Allie took the lead, directing the group back to the ramp. Although Drake did his best to keep up, he was unsteady at best. Geneva took him by the arm, and Allie slowed her pace. Instead of the quickest route, she found the one easiest to navigate with the least amount of debris and landscape to walk around.

"Hey. It looks like the Germans have some trouble, too," Ingrid said.

Allie, who had kept her focus on the path out, looked up and to her left and noticed the once-majestic, petrified tree had fallen during the quakes. Based on what she observed, at least one member of the German team looked trapped.

"Where did those three strong Australian guys go?" Ingrid asked.

"They probably ran right on by here without even pausing," Allie said. "Come on. Let's see if we can help."

As the group approached the Germans, they noticed Anna was the one missing.

"Need some assistance?" Allie said when they got to the site.

She didn't need an answer, because she saw with her own eyes what had happened. When the tree fell, the branches broke off first, and the trunk collapsed shortly after that. It had all fallen into one pile, and Anna, who had chased them away earlier in the day, got pinned inside a rough rectangle that resembled a coffin. There was a small triangle-shaped hole in the pile, and when Allie peered in, she caught Anna's scared face.

As Klaus barked orders, the three men of the German team were trying to move the top chunk of tree away from the pile, but were unable to do so. They ignored Allie and her friends, then Klaus shouted something else in German and the three men pushed, again with no results.

Rather than ask again, Allie motioned to her group to step in next to the Germans. Klaus counted in German and on three, the seven people strained to push the heavy stone. It rolled forward an inch, then settled back in place.

"Let's do it again," Allie said. "On my three."

Allie counted, and everyone pushed on her mark. This time, when the petrified tree trunk rolled forward, rather than hold back, the team pushed harder. The trunk hit another chunk and seemed like it would rock back, but the group gave it one last gasp and a final push, and the trunk rolled off the pile and landed on the ground, cracking in half when it did.

Allie looked down. There were two more sections of trunk on top of the pile. They were parallel and leaning against each other. The one closest to Allie was inches short of five feet long, the other was just over three feet long, but Allie recognized the problem with them right away. She moved to the hole and looked in. Anna was still there, looking like a caged animal. At best, she had only three feet of head clearance, so she reclined on her hip.

"Anna. We need to remove two more things before we can get you out. I don't know if we can move them both without one of them coming down on top of you. So here's my plan. We'll push the shorter one completely off and pull you out as fast as we can. See that piece above you to your left?"

Anna looked above her. "Yes."

"That's the one you should stay under. Get as far away from the other as you can, because I don't know if we can keep that one from falling in. You got me?"

"Yes," Anna said.

Anna crawled into position and flattened herself as much as possible next to the wall beneath the shorter tree segment.

Allie took a moment to study the people with her. Klaus, Jonas, and Felix, the German men, while not athletic looking in a conventional sense, all were larger in stature than anyone in her group, except Drake. She ran various combinations of people through her head, then finally came up with a game plan.

"Klaus, you, Drake and I will push away that smaller piece of the tree while everyone else keeps the larger piece from falling in. As soon as we move the tree away, you reach in and help

Anna get out of there. You'll need to hurry.

Allie expected an argument, but to her surprise, everyone seemed on board with the plan. Jonas and Ingrid and Felix and Geneva each stood against one end of the longer section, while Klaus and Drake took the shorter. Allie wedged in next to Drake, made sure everyone was ready, then gave the word to proceed.

Since she was unaccustomed to moving petrified trees, Allie had overestimated the weight of the smaller section and underestimated the weight of the larger one. The three of them easily moved their section, and the second they did, the larger piece started collapsing inward.

"Oh, crap!" Geneva said. "Allie, we're losing it!"

"Push harder!" Allie yelled.

In response Drake, Allie, and Klaus shoved the tree off of the pile, and the second it began its descent to the ground, Klaus and Drake turned around and added their muscle to the section that was slowly but surely on its way to crushing Anna.

"Anna, get up!" Allie screamed.

Anna's arm popped from below, and Allie grabbed Anna underneath her armpits and pulled her to her feet.

Allie winced at the sound of the scrape of stone on stone behind her and someone yelped in pain.

"We can't hold it!" Geneva said.

Allie glanced behind her and saw the tree was inches away from falling into the hole. She reached down, grabbed Anna by her belt, and in one motion hauled her from her tomb, pushed her over the side, and dropped her. Allie stepped aside from the pile and spun around just in time to see the tree segment crack in half, and both ends slide into the gap where Anna had been a few seconds before.

"Everyone okay?" Allie asked.

Felix held up his right hand, and Allie could see from a few feet away he had a dislocated little finger. She exhaled and moved over to his side.

"Let me take a gander at that. I'm a trained medic."

Felix nodded and let Allie have access to his hand.

Allie inspected it for a second. "Does it hurt?"

"*Ja,*" Felix said.

Allie took a closer look. "I never could figure out the difference between schnitzel and spaetzle. Do you know?"

A look of confusion passed over Felix's face, and he opened his mouth to answer, but before he could say anything, Allie grabbed the finger, pulled it, twisted it, and slid it back into place.

Felix howled for a second, and shook his hand in the air, trying to dispel the shock and pain.

"That's right. Schnitzel is meat. Spaetzle are noodles. Feel better?"

Felix stopped, then nodded.

The valley rumbled again, prompting everyone to walk toward the ramp. The valley protested further with every step they took, and when they finally climbed out of the pit, Allie looked around and realized one of the vehicles was gone, and Hap was sitting in his pickup waiting for them.

"Your friends took off in a big hurry," Hap said, addressing Ingrid. "What happened down there?"

Before Ingrid could respond, the valley groaned, and a sound echoed through the air that resembled the popping of a cork on a bottle of champagne. They heard a hiss and turned around as one just in time to see a large geyser erupt from the center of the valley. The white steam billowed against the bright blue sky, and the warm water fell back to earth, spraying them before running back into the valley.

"Never mind," Hap said, as he put his hands on his hips and watched the water flow.

CHAPTER SEVENTEEN

Geneva settled into a lounge chair poolside and kicked off her shoes. "Is anyone else tired of this?"

"Which part?" Drake asked. Thanks to a clinic a few blocks from the hotel, Drake sported a clean bandage on his head, under which the doctor had applied a liberal amount of surgical adhesive in lieu of stitches.

"The running all over the area and practically getting killed every day. I assumed this was supposed to be a nice, friendly geocaching competition, not an all out quest for survival."

Allie was doing slow laps in the swimming pool to work out the kinks in her muscles. She pulled her feet beneath her and used the stairs on the shallow end to leave the pool. Her towel was hanging on the back of her chair, and she retrieved it, made an effort to drip cool pool water on Drake, then wrapped the towel around her body and took her seat.

"This is turning out to be a lot more than we bargained for," Allie said. She ran the towel over her face and pushed her hair back. "We can't quit now, though. We need to see this thing through and figure out what it is we're really doing here."

"Still," Geneva said. "I could do with a day's rest."

Allie exhaled. "Me too. We all could, but that's a luxury I don't believe we have."

"Why not?" Drake said. "I imagine we were the only team that got what we needed at the valley. Neither of the other teams found what we did, and I would imagine that by now that valley is half-filled with water and no one will find those symbols without scuba gear and a lot of luck."

"I hate to admit it, but that's a good point Drake has. If the other teams didn't notice the symbols, they've got nothing to go on," Geneva said.

Allie considered the point and nodded.

The hotel door opened, and Ingrid walked out. She carried a piece of paper in her right hand and a wide grin on her face.

"I got it. This one I figured out all by myself."

"What?" Geneva asked.

"Where we need to go next," she said, holding out the paper. Allie took the sheet, folded it in half, then quarters before she handed it back to Ingrid. "Put that in your pocket. Where we're going next is anywhere we want to. Tomorrow's a free day."

Ingrid grinned. "Thank goodness."

* * *

When Allie woke the next morning, Ingrid was sitting by the desk, working her way through a paperback that she'd found in a nightstand drawer.

"Hey, you," Allie said. "What time is it?"

Ingrid turned around and smiled. "Good morning, sleepyhead. It's a little after eight. You slept hard last night."

Allie threw the covers back and sat up. "I was more tired than I thought. Give any consideration to what you want to do today?"

"I did, actually. There's a reptile center I'd like to visit, and right across the river from that are the botanic gardens we can wander through. I think there's a farmer's market nearby as well. If you wanted to, we could find any geocaches that might be along the way."

Allie nodded. "Okay. I'll go shower and then we can go. You know what Geneva and Drake are up to today?"

"Yeah. I got a text from her earlier. They plan on sleeping in and hanging around the pool today. Drake has quite the headache from yesterday."

"I'm not surprised. He took quite the whack on the noggin. I'm surprised he didn't get a concussion." Allie said. "It's a good day for some rest."

Allie showered and dressed, and she and Ingrid left the hotel by the main door. The reptile center was only a few blocks away, and after stopping to grab a pastry for breakfast, they headed there first. When they arrived, however, they found a handwritten sign on the front door that stated it was closed for the day. Directly across the street, they spotted the farmer's market in a park and decided to go there instead.

Dodging cars while jaywalking, they crossed the road. The second they stepped onto the safety of the sidewalk, Ingrid pulled her phone from her pocket and checked to see if there were any geocaches in the park.

"There's only one. It's two hundred feet that way," Ingrid said, pointing in the direction the arrow on the app dictated, which also matched the direction of where all the vendors had set up tents to sell their wares.

"Let's go then," Allie said.

Allie and Ingrid walked through the park, checking out each tent as they went to browse the items for sale. At one vendor, they stopped to inspect a selection of birdhouses crafted from wood, gourds, and other random materials.

Ingrid pointed out one that housed two nests in the design of a duplex house. "This is cute, isn't it? That guy whose finger you fixed yesterday is following us."

Allie examined the birdhouse closer, pointing out all the hand painted details, including a flower box with daisies, and individual bricks on the facade. "Where?"

"Two tents back, where the lady was selling honey products."

Allie moved around the tent, seemingly to check out other houses, but she positioned herself to see in the direction from which they'd come. Sure enough, Felix was near the honey seller, not at all interested in purchasing anything. "How far away is that cache yet?"

"A little over a hundred feet."

"Okay. Let's go for it and see if he follows."

Ingrid moved to the center aisle with Allie by her side, and together they bypassed the remaining vendors until they came to a group of three trees. Ingrid looked down at where the trunks of two of them met near the ground. Wedged between the trunks, she found a pill bottle wrapped in brown tape just a shade darker than the tree bark.

"Is he still there?" Ingrid asked as she pulled the log from the bottle and signed it. When she finished, she handed the paper and her pen to Allie.

"Yeah. He moved down to the far end of the tents, but slipped around to the back side. He's not good at surveillance if he's trying to spy on us. Felix sticks out like a sore thumb."

Allie handed the log back to Ingrid, who put the geocache back together, then replaced it where she'd found it. She stood erect, then rubbed her hands on her pants.

"His friend is on the other side," Ingrid said. "The one with the weird name."

"Lachlan?"

"That's it."

Allie directed her gaze to the vendor tents on the other side and noticed him right away. With his short dark brown hair and rugged and muscular frame, Lachlan wasn't hard to spot. "Maybe we should head back."

Ingrid didn't argue. Rather than walk through the farmer's market, they moved directly to the street and cut across it, stopping an oncoming Honda and receiving a wrong end of a blaring horn in the process. With haste, they rushed down a block, turned a corner, and jogged back to the hotel.

"Think they followed us?" Ingrid said as they approached their room. She dug her keycard out of her pocket and unlocked the door.

"I didn't see them. We should…"

Allie stopped talking the second she slipped through the door and gasped when she noticed the condition of their room. Someone had gone through everything. The sheets were off the bed, the dresser drawers pulled out and dumped on the floor, and every article of clothing appeared strewn about.

"What happened here?" Allie asked.

Ingrid shrugged. "Either the housekeeper had a terrible day, or someone has robbed us."

Allie and Ingrid spent an hour putting the room back together and found nothing missing.

"What were they looking for?" Allie asked as she shoved the last drawer into the dresser.

Ingrid removed a paper from her rear pocket. "Probably this."

* * *

Ingrid pulled out of the hotel parking lot at just after four in the morning. Allie rode shotgun. Tucked comfortably in the backseat, Geneva and Drake had fallen asleep by the time Ingrid passed the city limits sign.

The moon was low, and the stars dotted the sky like Christmas lights. Allie tinkered with the radio, found a station that featured American classic country music, and turned the volume down.

"Are you sure we're headed for the right place?" Allie asked.

Ingrid smiled, although no one could spot it in the dark. "Yep. As sure as I'm sitting here. The symbols clearly spelled out the location as Lake Amadeus as easy as if written in English. There are little islands on the lake, and I believe the next set of clues, if not the stone, is somewhere on one of those islands."

"It sounds like that will take forever to search," Allie said.

"Not as long as you might think. There are several islands, but I've narrowed it down to four or five, and they're fairly close together."

"I don't suppose you know where we'll be able to rent a boat?"

"We won't need to worry about a boat. The lake is only a few inches deep this time of year."

"How long until we get there?"

Ingrid checked the GPS on top of the dashboard. "Five hours or so."

Allie nodded, turned the volume up on the radio so she wouldn't fall asleep, and stared out the window, watching the miles roll by.

Forty-five minutes later, Allie opened her eyes. She checked the GPS arrival time and realized she'd fallen asleep despite her best efforts not to. She glanced over at Ingrid, who appeared to be wide awake and doing well. A glance in the rear-view told her that Geneva and Drake were still sound asleep. Next, she looked out the side mirror and noticed two sets of headlights behind them.

"We've got company?" Allie asked.

Ingrid looked over at her friend and smiled. "Hello. Did you have a nice nap?"

"Sorry. I didn't mean to fall asleep on you."

"It's fine. I expected you to. Yes. Those cars have been with us since we left the hotel. I think it's our geocaching friends."

Allie rolled her eyes. "The friends that followed us yesterday, and set a tornado loose in our hotel room?"

"Those are the ones."

"Do you think you can lose them?"

Ingrid shook her head. "Where? It's literally two paved roads from here to the lake, and I'm certainly not going to go down some dusty farm road in the dark."

"Good point," Allie said.

"We'll find out if it's them in another hour and a quarter when I stop for gas and a bathroom break," Ingrid said.

An hour later, Ingrid saw the lights of a service station and pulled off the highway and up to a pump. While Allie got out to pump the gas, Ingrid rousted Geneva and Drake from their sleep. By the time they were all out of the Jeep, both the Australian and German geocaching teams pulled into the station.

"Morning. Lovely day for a drive, isn't it?" Ethan said as he approached Allie.

"Where'd you come from?" Allie asked.

"We were wondering if you'd like to team up for this next stage," Ethan said, ignoring her question.

"What makes you think we're looking for the next stage? We're just out for a drive." Allie turned her attention to the pump, willing the gas to flow faster so she could get out of there.

Ethan shrugged. "Just a wild guess is all. We don't think you'd leave town so early without a specific location in mind. We'd like to tag along if it's okay with you."

"And what if it isn't okay?" Drake said. He stepped in front of Allie, effectively putting himself between Allie and Ethan.

Ethan grinned. "The sheila needs to have her man step in to protect her?"

"No, mate," Drake said. "I stepped in to protect you from her. We don't want you following us."

Ethan rolled his eyes, which they easily caught under the

bright lights of the service station. "It doesn't matter what you want. It's a free country, and we're going to be right on your tail until you get to where you're going."

Allie saw the muscles in Drake's neck tense up, so she knew he was about to get himself into trouble, so she wrapped her arms around him and whispered into his ear. "Let it go, Drake. Step away."

Drake held his position for a moment, then shook his head and walked toward the building.

"All right then," Ethan said. "We'll get some petrol, grab some snacks, and get back on the road then."

Ethan waved, turned, and headed into the building.

Allie let out a verbal growl.

"Someone's not happy," Ingrid said.

"Those guys have a lot of nerve," Allie said. "It was bad enough they didn't even thank us for getting them out of trouble the other day, but now they want to jump in on our act."

The handle clicked, so Allie put it back on the pump and closed the gas cap.

"Do you need anything from inside?" Ingrid asked.

Allie shook her head and when Ingrid headed off to use the ladies' room, Allie jumped back into the Jeep. She checked the GPS and saw there were just a little over two hours left to go before they got to the lake. She put her head against the window and closed her eyes.

"Allie?"

Allie felt someone pushing on her shoulder and opened her eyes. She looked over and realized Ingrid was waking her. The Jeep had stopped moving.

"We're here," Ingrid said.

Allie rubbed her eyes and looked out the window. Not only had she slept away the entire rest of the ride, but she'd missed the sunrise as well. It was still low in the sky, so she knew they had plenty of daylight to find what they came for. Allie jumped from the Jeep and went around to the back to retrieve her pack. While she was waiting for Drake to pass them out, she watched as the Australians and Germans parked nearby.

"What's the plan?" Geneva asked as the four huddled around the Jeep's rear bumper.

Ingrid pulled the paper from her pocket and flipped it over. On the back she'd made a crude map of Lake Amadeus, including a half-dozen islands she'd drawn in with coordinates written on them.

"The symbols didn't point me to a specific island, but more a group of them. I used a map to determine the coordinates of the center of four of them. We can either explore each island together before moving on, or we can each take one and search on our own. Which way should we go?"

"Why don't we split into pairs?" Geneva asked. "That way, we would have another set of eyes on each island and still cover more ground than as one large group."

"Works for me," Ingrid said. "Anyone opposed?"

No one said a word, so Allie and Ingrid and Drake and Geneva paired off. Ingrid shared her coordinates with Geneva, and they each selected an island to start on and headed toward the lake.

Allie and Ingrid crested a small hill and spotted the lake below them. Allie wasn't sure how large the lake was, but it was long enough that it carried all the way to the horizon. A few yards ahead, Drake and Geneva had already reached the waterline, and both were taking off their boots and socks and rolling up their pant legs.

Allie heard a noise behind her, stopped, looked back toward the vehicles, and saw the seven other geocachers only a few feet from them. The Australians rushed past the couple and followed Drake and Geneva into the water.

Allie and Ingrid made their way to the shore.

"How deep is it?" Allie asked.

Ingrid shrugged and stepped into the water. It barely made it past the soles of her hiking boots. Undaunted, she checked her phone, turned her body slightly, and headed off on an angle to the southwest of Drake and Geneva. Allie checked to make sure her laces were tight, then followed a few paces behind Ingrid.

Allie heard a splash behind her and glanced back. The German team had followed them, and they kept pace as one group before Anna and Felix broke off from the others and headed off toward an island with no other groups on it. Allie traipsed for a hundred yards before she reached the shore of the island, climbed over a small berm, and stood on dry land once again. She looked for Drake and Geneva and saw they had also made it to their island, only a few hundred yards away. The Australians had caught up to them, and all five people had started a search of that little patch of land.

Allie looked at the island, and noticed it wasn't that large at all, only half the size of a football field, and consisted primarily of bedrock covered in several places with either piles of rocks, or places where the ancient sea had dropped, leaving behind a short pillar or mound of the same rock she stood on. Vegetation was practically non-existent, and on this particular island, there stood only one tree that was barely as tall as she was.

Ingrid rushed toward the tree with Klaus only a few yards behind her. Allie understood the logic, but she guessed the answer would be in the rock formations, if they found the answer at all. She watched as Ingrid checked the tree, then Ingrid turned and jogged back to Allie's side.

"Find a cache?" Allie asked.

"No. Just trying to mess with our friend," Ingrid said, shaking a thumb toward the tree.

While Ingrid had given the tree only a cursory look, the German was spending much more time and effort on it.

"Good job. Although it will be hard to hide anything we find out here," Allie said.

Ingrid shrugged. "Doesn't hurt to try. Where should we look first?"

CHAPTER EIGHTEEN

Allie and Ingrid had checked their little island from one end of the other and found nothing more than naturally occurring rock formations. Klaus and Jonas, the Germans searching the same patch of land they were hadn't found anything either, so when the women moved on to their next island, the men followed them almost step for step.

Allie had kept her eye on Anna and Felix, Drake and Geneva, and the Australian team. Drake and Geneva had finished with their island not long after Allie had begun her trek across the lake. The Australians followed her friends, and the Germans were still off doing their own thing.

Allie removed the pack from her back, and from it withdrew a bottle of water.

"I think it's going to be a hot one today," she said, passing Ingrid the bottle.

Ingrid took a swig and passed the bottle back. "It already is. And it's not even noon yet."

Allie stuffed the water into her pack and let the pack fall to her feet. "At least there's a place to swim."

Ingrid grinned. "And how does one swim in two inches of water? Lay down and roll over?"

Allie considered the point. "Okay. Maybe swim is the wrong word to use in this case. How are our friends doing?"

Ingrid spun and looked behind her. Klaus and Jonas were investigating a rock formation that Allie had checked only a few minutes before. "Still right behind us, hoping to uncover something that we missed."

"Did we miss anything?" Allie asked.

"I'd say no, but I'm not a hundred percent convinced we know what we're looking for," Ingrid said.

Allie conceded the point. She moved on to the next rock formation, which was the approximate shape and height of a fire hydrant. Allie crouched, and carefully inspected the rock, looking for any carving or marking that appeared to be manmade. Once she'd circled the formation and found nothing visible, she went around again, this time exploring any holes or indentations in the stone and on the ground around its base. As a last-ditch attempt, she tried to move the stone, but it wouldn't budge. She exhaled loud and long, picked up her pack, and moved on to the next stone where Ingrid was already hard at work.

"It's not here, either," Ingrid said. "Did we miss anything on this island?"

Allie scanned the area. "No. We looked everywhere."

Ingrid took the paper from her pocket and from it entered the coordinates for the fifth island into her phone. "It's got to be this one, then. Let's go."

As Ingrid and Allie marched across the lake to their next island, Drake and Geneva joined them about halfway. No one spoke until they got to land.

"Are you sure we're in the right place?" Geneva asked.

Ingrid was about to defend her mapping skills when an enormous cheer erupted.

Allie pivoted and spotted Anna and Felix on the next island over, jumping to get the attention of their comrades. Klaus and Jonas, who were on the way to the island that Allie was on, turned around in their tracks and headed off to join their friends.

The four Germans huddled around a rock formation that had an unnatural hump in the middle. Anna took several photographs of the rock, then stepped back. Klaus removed a couple of things from his backpack and stepped up to the rock and began to destroy it using a hammer and chisel.

"Hey, they can't do that!" Drake protested when he noticed what was happening.

"They're doing it," Geneva said morosely.

Klaus gave the rock another whack, and the rock fell apart. Satisfied, the Germans all got to their feet and began running across the lake to the mainland. The Australians took off in chase.

"Now what? Should we follow?" Geneva asked.

Ingrid removed the paper from her pocket and studied it. "It doesn't make sense. There shouldn't be anything on that island. I'm going to go take a look."

Ingrid crossed over to the other island, her friends right behind her, and approached the destroyed rock formation. "Think we can piece this back together?" she asked as she knelt at the pile.

Her friends began collecting pieces of rock and began putting the formation back together, not unlike building a 3D jigsaw puzzle.

* * *

Jonas checked the side mirror and noticed a large plume of dust in the sky, indicating that the Australians had reached their vehicle and were speeding down the dirt road toward them.

The Germans were in better physical shape and had no problem winning the footrace from the island to the cars, and although Anna suggested disabling the other vehicles there, they didn't want to waste the time. Instead, they'd gotten into their SUV and Jonas and stomped on the accelerator.

"They're gaining," Klaus yelled in German.

"I see them," Jonas said.

The road, such as it was, seemed nothing more than a set of tire tracks that had run from the main highway for fifteen miles until they reached the lake. The SUV bounced along as Jonas tried to keep the car aligned with the ruts.

"Faster!" Anna ordered.

Despite his better judgment, Jonas stepped on the accelerator and the needle on the speedometer rose steadily. He hit a dip in the road, one that caused the SUV to go airborne for a second before bouncing on the ground and jumping again before settling back into the tire tracks.

Jonas checked the mirror again and to his horror he saw the Australians right on his tail. His eyes widened as he saw the car behind them inch forward, and a second later, he slammed his head against the window as the SUV bounced toward the sky.

Lachlan had caught up to the Germans and, with one deft maneuver, tapped the rear quarter panel right behind the tire. The Germans' SUV skidded sideways for a second, hit a large rock, then flipped in the air three times before settling on its hood. They'd landed on the crest of a steep hill and teetered there. Lachlan stopped the vehicle, and the three Australians got out and approached the Germans.

"You've got yourself in a bit of a spot," Ethan said. He knelt next to the driver's door and looked in.

All the windows had busted. Jonas had a face full of blood from an apparent broken nose. Anna, who was in the passenger seat, had a large bleeding cut across her forehead. They both dangled upside-down. Felix and Klaus had not remembered to buckle up in the backseat, so they were both unconscious, their bodies intermingled on the roof, which was now the floor.

"Here's my offer. You hand us the phone, unlocked, and we help you out of here. You don't give us the phone, we slide you down the hill," Ethan said.

Jonas blinked a few times, trying hard to stay awake. "Phone?"

"Yeah, mate. The phone. You give us the pictures you shot of the rock. We save your lives. Fair trade, I think."

"Anna. Give me your phone," Jonas said.

Anna pulled the phone from her pocket, unlocked it, and handed it to Jonas, who passed it to Ethan.

Ethan looked at the pictures and nodded. "Excellent decision, mate. Boys, help these people out."

Ethan got to his feet and stepped back. At the rear of the SUV, Lachlan and Jack lifted the back bumper as they pushed. It took little for the vehicle to overcome the pivot point and for gravity to take over. The SUV started to slide on its hood, slowly at first, then picked up speed as it slid down the slope. The Australians watched as it disappeared from view. Ethan handed the phone to Lachlan.

Lachlan glanced at the pictures, then swore. "Those German fools," he said.

* * *

"I've got it!" Geneva said. She stood up and waved her hands in the air. "A point goes to Ingrid for recognizing those markings as coming from fossils and not etchings. I still can't believe the Germans made that mistake."

"I would've too had I been in a hurry and not patient enough to verify what I found," Ingrid said.

"Take a look at this," Geneva said. Her friends quickly gathered around the two-foot square by three-foot high rock formation she'd been studying.

"Where?" Allie asked

"Here. At the base of this stone. It runs around all the sides. It's hard to see, but if you run your fingers on it, you can tell there's a distinctive pattern."

Allie did as Geneva suggested and nodded. "There's something here. We should get a rubbing to see it better."

Ingrid set her backpack down and dug into it for a few seconds, then came out with a notepad and a pencil. "I got this."

Allie and Geneva stepped back from the stone while Ingrid transferred the images from the stone to her paper.

"This doesn't seem right," Allie said when Ingrid handed her a completed sheet. "These appear to be half there."

Ingrid glanced at the sheet she had just finished and handed it to Allie. "I guess you're right." She bent over close to the where the rock met the ground, almost touching her nose to the earth. Ingrid felt the ground with her fingertips, then gently blew away a layer of dirt and dust. "There's more down here."

Ingrid found some fresh sheets of paper and made a second trip around the stone, this time concentrating on the marks on the ground. Since caked-in dirt made many unreadable, the team needed to dig them out the best they could before Ingrid could take a rubbing of them.

When she finished, they had two complete sets of symbols, and it became a simple matter of aligning the top and bottom halves to get the message. The symbols repeated four times, making the message seem longer than it actually was.

"I've seen this before," Ingrid said.

Ingrid dug her phone out of her pocket and started scrolling through screens.

"You actually have service out here?" Drake asked.

"No," Ingrid said without looking up. "I found myself referencing the same material over and over again during the last week, so I downloaded all the pages I used the most."

She scrolled through page after page until she finally found the one she needed. "Okay. I know where we need to go."

Ingrid started walking off, with Geneva right behind her.

"Wait!" Drake said. "We should try to obscure these markings in case the others come back."

"Good idea," Allie said.

While Drake and Allie pressed the dirt around the base of the stone back into the ground, Geneva and Ingrid used lake water and dirt to make a paste that they used to hide the marks on the stone itself. Satisfied that everything would dry quickly under the desert sun, the four left the island with haste and headed back to their Jeep.

"Everyone strapped in?" Ingrid asked.

Ingrid hit the gas without waiting for an answer, then did a U-turn and headed away from the lake. She drove for a half mile and came to a fork in the road.

"Anyone remember which way we came in?" Ingrid asked.

"Ha, ha, Ingrid," Geneva said. "Let's stop wasting time."

"Um, I'm not kidding." Ingrid parked the Jeep and glanced at Allie.

"Don't look at me. I was sleeping when we arrived, remember?"

Ingrid peered into the rearview. Geneva shook her head, and Drake had a lost expression on his face. She sighed and stepped out of the Jeep and walked a few yards down in each direction. They looked the same to her, so she returned to her seat.

"Okay, on the count of three, everyone hold up a random number of fingers from one to five. One, two, three."

Allie, Geneva, and Drake all held up their fingers. Ingrid counted them and came up with a total.

"Ten. That's an even number, so we'll go right," Ingrid said, putting the Jeep into gear and making the turn.

* * *

Ten minutes later, Lachlan returned to the location where

they'd parked when they accessed the lake and found the area empty.

"Are we in the right place?" Ethan asked.

Lachlan opened the door, stepped out for a second, then took his seat. "This is the place. There are three sets of tire tracks here."

"We must have missed them," Ethan said.

Lachlan rolled his eyes. "You think?"

Lachlan put his Jeep into gear, turned around, and headed away. A half mile later, he stopped at the same fork Ingrid had. "They must have gone out the other way."

"So now we're faced with a decision," Jack said. "We either run them down and see what they found, or we follow them."

Lachlan thought it over for a few moments. "I think we should follow them. If they're already gone, they must have found whatever was out there and had an idea where they're headed. We'll hang back and see where they're going next."

* * *

Ingrid realized she'd made a mistake and had gotten them lost when she came to another fork in the road. This time, instead of two choices to make, she had three.

"Any ideas, Allie?" Ingrid said.

"Who has the map?" Allie asked.

"It's here," Geneva said. She pulled it from the pocket behind Ingrid's seat and passed it forward.

Allie studied it for a moment, found their approximate location and placed her index finger on the map. "Which way is east?"

Geneva brought up a compass app on her phone, then passed the phone to Allie. Allie compared the compass to the map and looked at the road options in front of her.

"Let's take the road that goes straight. That will take us in the general direction of the highway. As long as we keep going east, we'll hit the road at some point."

Without another question, Ingrid motored on straight ahead. Allie kept an eye on the map while Ingrid focused on the road ahead, and together they stayed on an easterly heading, and, after an hour, the road turned from worn dirt tire tracks to a paved highway.

"Which way?" Allie asked. "Left will take us back to Alice Springs, I think."

"Then I think we need to go right," Ingrid said.

"Why? Where are we headed?"

"I'll give you a hint. What's big and rocky and red all over?" Ingrid asked.

"Ayers Rock?" Geneva said.

"The former Ayers Rock," Ingrid said. "It reverted to its original name of Uluru. Yes, that's where we're going. Allie, can you do the honors and enter it into the GPS?"

Allie did. "It's less than an hour from here."

"That's good, because I think it will take us a while to find what we need," Ingrid said as she turned right onto the highway. "If I'm reading the symbols correctly, we need to find an entrance hidden in the shadow of the red mountain."

"How big is Uluru?" Drake asked.

"Oh, about two and a half miles long and a over a mile wide," Ingrid said.

Drake groaned. "That's a lot of potential ground to cover." Allie nodded. "Maybe. But there might be a way to narrow it down. They have walking trails and a visitor center. We could probably pick up a map of the entire location and all the trails. We could probably eliminate any areas that are heavily hiked, or any natural tourist site, like a spring or whatever."

"Why?" Drake asked.

"Because if the entrance was near one of those, someone would have discovered it years ago," Allie said.

"We've got company again," Ingrid said. "Our friends, the

Australians, are following us again."

"Ugh," Allie said. "Don't they have places of their own to go?"

"They took off after the German team. Any sign of them?" Drake asked.

Ingrid checked her rearview and then her side mirror. "Doesn't look like it. There's only one car behind us. Should I pull over and we can say hello?"

Allie shook her head. "Not worth it. Keep going. Since we're going to Uluru, we can play it off as a simple recreational visit. After all, it is the most famous tourist site in this part of the country."

"All right then," Ingrid said. "Simple tourists we are."

Ingrid kept her speed at a steady five kilometers over the speed limit, and the Australians kept a consistent distance behind them. Forty minutes later, Ingrid pulled into the parking lot of the cultural center and shut down the Jeep.

As a group, they stopped at the restrooms before going on to the cultural center, which turned out to be part museum, part workshop, with a gift store and a cafe thrown in for good measure. Drake hit the small restaurant for a snack, and Ingrid checked out the shop while Geneva and Allie visited the museum.

From where Drake sat at a table waiting for the others while eating an ice cream bar, he easily spotted Lachlan as he slipped into the museum, and Jack as he stepped into the store. Ethan, it seemed, had a sudden urge to drink a bottle of soda and eat a Hershey bar.

"Can I have a bite of that?" Ingrid asked when she joined Drake at his table.

"Nope," Drake said. "You can get your own, though."

"Such a nice guy," she teased.

Drake reached into his pocket and pulled out a few Australian dollars and handed them to Ingrid. "Here. I'm buying.

Get something refreshing and come back here and wait for the others. I'm going to head over to the park headquarters and see if they have a map."

"What about our Australian friends?" Ingrid asked.

"I assume one of them will follow me and the other will stay here with you. I'd say don't engage with them unless they come up and start talking to you. Otherwise, just enjoy whatever treat you get and wait for the girls. I'll be back in a few minutes."

"And then what?" Ingrid asked.

"Then we have to see if there's a way to shake these guys."

CHAPTER NINETEEN

"Are they still behind us?" Geneva asked as she adjusted the straps of her backpack. When she finished, she put her hand back into Drake's.

Drake turned and glanced behind his group. Only a few yards to the rear of them, the Australians kept pace. "Yep."

"What should we do about that?" Geneva asked.

Drake pointed to a covered picnic table not far ahead. "Let's have a seat in the shade and take a break."

The group hiked the path until they got to a small picnic area and slid into seats on the wooden table only fifty yards from the famous monolith. Behind them, the massive red sandstone monolith rose eleven-hundred feet above the ground. Although there were plenty of tourists already hiking the trails, the number of people would triple at sunset when Uluru would shift to vibrant hues of crimson and orange.

"Okay, who has a plan?" Drake asked.

"I thought you did," Geneva said.

Allie pulled out her map and checked where they were on the trail. After a few seconds, she spotted the picnic area and examined the rest of the route. She looked over her shoulder to determine where the Australians were and spotted them two tables over, all sitting in a way to watch Allie and her friends. Allie stood, knelt on the bench, put her map in the middle of the table and leaned over it so no one other than the people she was with could see anything.

"We're here," Allie said, pointing at their current location. "Based on Ingrid's message, I think the most likely places to find a secret entrance are here, along the far side, and in here, where the trail veers away from the mountain."

"Great. But how does that help us lose our buddies over there?" Drake asked.

"There are four of us, three of them. We should break up and each of us head in a separate direction. Whoever doesn't have a tail goes to where we think the entrance may be, whoever gets a follower does whatever they can to lose the tail and meet up here," Allie said, pointing to a spot on the map. "If the plan falls apart and we can't lose them, or they get wise to us, we'll all meet back at the car in two hours and try again tomorrow."

As one, the group rose from the table. Geneva and Allie backtracked to the trail they'd come on, acting as if they were returning to the parking area. As they walked past the Australians, Jack and Ethan got to their feet and followed them again, staying a few paces behind. Drake and Ingrid continued on the trail they'd not yet explored, with Lachlan following them.

Drake and Ingrid followed the trail until they came to a fork. To their left, the path led through a gorge to a natural spring.
"I think I'm going to check this out. Want to come?" Drake said, a little louder than necessary to make sure Lachlan overheard him.

"Nah," Ingrid said. "I'm going to keep going or I'll never finish the loop."

"Good luck," Drake whispered.

"You too."

Drake broke to the left, picked up his pace, and headed away. Ingrid pulled a bottle of water from her pack and took a drink, hesitating long enough to see which choice Lachlan would make. He made eye contact with Ingrid for ten seconds and headed down the trail to catch up with Drake. Ingrid grinned, stowed her bottle, and jogged along the path.

Ingrid consulted her copy of the map, and when she got close to the area where Allie believed the entrance may be, she left the dirt trail and angled in to be close to the rock. Once there, she hiked along the base of Uluru on the lookout for anything she could find that might serve as a way into the mountain.

"Hey," Ingrid heard a few feet behind her. She turned and saw Geneva had caught up with her.

"Hey yourself," Ingrid said. "How did you get away?"

"I went to the bathroom. Turns out it has inside and outside entrances, so I slipped into the building to go in, and he followed me inside. I walked right out the other door, stealthily moved around to the other side of the building and came here."

"Did you see Allie or Drake?"

Geneva shook her head. "How are things going here?"

"I haven't found anything yet, but I'm glad to have another set of eyes."

Together, the friends resumed their search, and after hiking a mile, they'd found nothing. Geneva had found one fissure in the surface of the rock large enough to enter, but when she entered, it ended abruptly. At mile two, Allie caught up to the pair, and a mile later, Drake appeared.

"What about up there?" Geneva said, pointing to an area where two sizeable areas that looked like domes came together and created a narrow valley in the center. The dome on the left had a large section the shape of a football missing from the side, making the dome appear like it had a large cave for a mouth. Enormous boulders, some twenty feet tall, had slid to the bottom of the mountain, looking like discarded teeth.

"The middle or the cave?" Drake asked.

"Either one."

"Looks pretty steep. Think we can get up there?"

"I don't know, but that cave's in the shade, so my guess would be there," Geneva said.

Drake nodded. "Okay. I'll go check it out."

As Drake approached the slope and tried to determine his best way up, Allie took off her backpack and stepped into the shade made by a thirty-foot-high boulder that had cracked in half when it impacted the ground. She was about to sit when she spotted a snake headed straight toward her. Allie stepped aside and watched as the serpent slithered into the crack. When Allie stepped closer to the rock to determine if she could spot where it disappeared to, she got a surprise.

"Hey. There are stairs here," she said.

Allie moved around to the far side of the boulder, where the crack expanded from a few inches to a few feet wide, then stepped forward. There, cut into the sandstone, was a set of stairs.

"Where do they go?" Ingrid asked as she stepped behind Allie.

"They go down," Allie said. "Go tell Drake to come back if he hasn't already made it to the top."

"Top? He's still thinking about his first step," Ingrid said. She called for Drake, and Drake and Geneva joined them.

"Should we go down?" Ingrid asked.

Allie, closest to the stairs, hesitated at the top. "I'm not sure."

Drake pushed his way past Ingrid and Geneva and put his hand on Allie's shoulder. "I have a better idea. Why don't you stand guard up here and make sure nothing happens? We'll go and be back in no time."

Geneva nodded in agreement. "That's a good idea. We need someone up here in case we don't come back. You can go for help. If we're not back in like three hours, call in the rangers."

Allie hesitantly agreed, then stepped away from the stairs so the others could pass. She watched as, one by one, they disappeared into the darkness, then found a seat in the shade and began waiting.

* * *

They stopped on the thirtieth step to push away a large rock that had settled on the stairs, then descended twenty more until the stairs ended and they found themselves in a long corridor. Drake took the lead and walked fifty paces until the corridor ended at a junction.

"Left or right?" Drake asked.

"Hold on." Ingrid dug out the impressions of the symbols, aligned the papers, and studied them for a moment. "See here, above each symbol there's a line cut, along with a crude dot?"

Geneva and Drake focused their flashlight beams on the paper.

"Yeah?" Geneva said.

"I thought whatever tool they used to etch the markings into the stone made these marks, but what if they're actually directions and the dot tells us which way to go?" Ingrid said.

"You said those symbols repeated. How would you know where to start?" Drake asked.

Ingrid shuffled through the papers. "Check this out. A long line followed by a short vertical line and a short horizontal line. What does that seem like to you?"

"Stairs?" Drake asked.

Ingrid smiled. "Stairs. So, based on the pattern, we should turn right here."

"Are you sure we're not going to go around in circles down here?" Geneva asked.

"No," Drake said. Rather than explain, he moved to the wall on the right side and made two small piles of stone, one in the long corridor, and one around the corner. "If we get lost, we can follow these back."

"Great idea," Geneva said. "Now that we know how to get to where we're going, let's get a move on. I don't want to spend any more time down here than necessary."

* * *

Allie heard voices and opened her eyes. She mentally kicked herself for falling asleep at her post, but the long walk and desert heat had done her in.

"Are you sure they came this way?" Jack said.

"There are tracks right there, as plain as day," Ethan said.

Allie got to her feet and slowly looked around the rock that shielded her from the men. Sure enough, the Australians were on their trail. Allie looked at the ground and realized they'd left enough footprints in the sand for a Cub Scout to track. She mentally kicked herself again. Realizing they'd find her, Allie determined her only option was to hide behind a nearby rock. Slowly and walking backward, she moved away from the entrance and headed for the nearest place to seek refuge.

* * *

Ingrid used a pencil to check each turn off the paper as they made them. After eighteen turns, they came to the remains of a bridge that spanned a chasm. Drake stepped to the edge and shined his light into the hole, and he didn't see the bottom. Instead, he kicked a stone into the void and waited. After seven seconds, he caught a dim clatter when it hit bottom.

"Don't tell me we need to get across this," Geneva said.

Ingrid consulted her map. "Straight across and turn left and we're there."

"How far is it across?" Geneva asked.

Drake shined his light to the other side. "Not far. Six, maybe seven feet."

"Great. Might as well be a million," Geneva said.

"We can just take the bridge," Drake pointed out. "It may not look like much, but it looks okay to me."

The three shined their lights on the footbridge. There were several places where the wood plank decking was missing, and there was no telling what condition the supports were in. Handrails didn't exist.

"You really think that's safe?" Ingrid asked.

"Not a chance in hell," Drake said. "But what choice do we have? Come back tomorrow with safety gear?"

Without waiting, Drake moved to the bridge and stepped on the first plank. It creaked but held his weight. He put his other foot down and sighed when the board supported his body. He took another step forward, but when he tried to bring over the next foot, the bridge swayed.

"Ah, no," Drake said.

Slowly, Drake got to his knees, then spread out his hands. Staying as close to the boards and as wide as possible, he slowly crawled across the bridge. When he got to the other side, he got to his feet and grinned. "See. Nothing to it."

* * *

Jack, Lachlan, and Ethan followed the corridor until they came to the end.

"Which way?" Lachlan said.

Ethan and Jack each selected a different direction, walked a few feet, then returned. As he pivoted, Jack's flashlight beam came to rest on a small pile of stones.

"Hey, look at that," Jack said.

* * *

Ingrid, Geneva, and Drake turned the last corner and entered a ten-foot-square room. In the center of the room stood eight stone altars. On each altar sat a stone the size of a volleyball.

"Holy cow," Drake said. "Is one of these the stone?"

Ingrid flashed her light around the room and noticed there were four additional altars along the back wall, but a minor ceiling cave in had toppled them all. The stones were on the floor, and one had cracked in half. Bright purple appeared when she shined her light on the rock.

"Hey. Is this an amethyst?" she asked.

Geneva joined her, crouched, and handled the stone. "It's a geode."

"There's another one over here," Drake said, standing over the next fallen altar. "The mysterious stone of the Rainbow Serpent is just a geode?"

Ingrid wandered around the room, feeling each geode as she went. She was on her fifth when something seemed different.

"Come over here," she said.

As Drake and Geneva drew close, Ingrid put her hands on either side of the stone. It started to glow under her touch.

"That's not a geode," Drake said. "That has to be it. Is it hot?"

Ingrid shook her head. "Cold, actually." She tried to lift it and found it to be light, like hefting a foam ball. "This is amazing."

As she held the stone, it glowed brighter and pulsated. A second later it changed to white, then to red, orange, and violet in successive order.

"You should put that thing down. It might be radioactive," Drake said.

Ingrid nodded and set the stone back on the altar. The second she removed her hands, the light stopped, and it transformed back to looking like every other geode in the room.

"Let's check the rest of them," Geneva said.

The group circled the room, laying hands on each geode, but

nothing responded the way the one Ingrid had found did. She moved back to the stone and stashed it in her backpack.

"Let's get out of here," Geneva said once Ingrid donned her backpack.

The group left the room, and with the aid of Drake's piles of stones, quickly found their way back to the bridge. Using the same careful method as they used to traverse it the first time, Ingrid crossed first. She took a few steps forward to get out of the way of the others, then stopped and listened for a moment.

She rushed back to the bridge. "There are voices. I think there are people coming," she said, just loud enough for Drake and Geneva to hear.

"Ditch your backpack!" Drake said.

Ingrid spun in a quick circle, trying to find a place to stash her backpack. Finding no large rocks, holes in the wall, or a quick way to dangle it from the bridge, she ran down the passage a few feet to where the junction was. She looked to the left, to the direction from which they came, and saw the dim beam of a moving flashlight. Ingrid turned right instead, counted off fifteen paces, then dropped her backpack on the ground and made it as flat as possible. She felt dirt under her hands, so she gathered what she could and threw it over the pack, hoping to make it less noticeable if anyone came in that direction. Sensing she'd done all that she could at the moment, she backtracked to the bridge. She was about to cross when she heard a voice behind her.

"Hold on there, sheila."

Ingrid turned around and got a face full of light for her trouble. She held up her hand to block the beam.

"Where are you going?" Lachlan said. "Across the bridge, is that it? Go on, don't let us stop you."

Ingrid wanted to respond, but Jack spun her around by the shoulders and hit her on the butt like she was a stubborn mule that refused to move. She took the hint, stepped onto the bridge, and slowly made her way across, followed closely by the three men.

"Where to next?" Ethan asked.

"Right around the corner," Ingrid said.

"Go," Lachlan said.

Drake got in front of Ingrid and Geneva and stood chest to chest with Lachlan. "Screw you. We're leaving!"

Lachlan made a swift move, and Drake saw a glint of steel, then screamed when he felt a blade slice across his left arm just above his elbow.

"Go," Lachlan repeated. "The next one won't be quite so nice."

"This way," Ingrid said, walking away without waiting. Geneva and Drake followed, Drake holding his arm.

When they got to the alter room, Lachlan pushed the friends into a corner, gave Jack his knife and had him stand guard.

"Can I look at his wound?" Geneva asked.

When Jack didn't answer, Geneva took that as a go-ahead.

"Ingrid, can you shine your light over here?"

Ingrid did as Geneva asked, and Geneva lifted Drake's shirt sleeve and spotted a five-inch vertical line of blood that began just above Drake's elbow and traced the side of his bicep.

"We need to put something on this," Geneva said. She slid off her backpack, and from within pulled her water bottle, which she used to rinse the wound. She had a spare pair of clean socks, so she fashioned one into a makeshift bandage and secured it with a length of parachute cord from her backpack.

"Not bad," Drake whispered. "Allie would be proud."

"Shh," Geneva said. "Just try to relax."

"Look at this," Lachlan said, approaching Jack with a half of the amethyst geode. "This will be worth some money. There's a citrine, too, and Ethan found a sapphire the size of a chicken egg. It looks like we found the treasure, mate. Let's load up our packs and go. Get their packs, too."

"What should we do with them?" Jack asked.

"Tie them up or something and leave them here," Lachlan said.

Lachlan stepped away, and Jack turned his attention back to his charges. "Empty the packs," he ordered.

Geneva dumped out the contents of her backpack, and Ingrid helped Drake out of his and spilled the contents onto the ground. Drake carried a length of parachute cord, too, and Jack used it to tie the hands of Geneva, Ingrid, and Drake behind them, then secured all their wrists together so they sat bunched together in a triangle.

Jack picked up the empty backpacks and joined the others, gathering up the geodes and dividing them among themselves.

The task complete, Lachlan approached the Americans. "Well, it's been fun. You can have the place to yourselves now." He noticed three flashlights laying on the floor, took them, and shoved them into his pack. "See you later."

Lachlan, Jack, and Ethan left the chamber, taking all the flashlights with them.

"Well, crap," Drake said. "Anyone have a light?"

CHAPTER TWENTY

Allie moved back to the stairs the moment the third man slipped down into the darkness. She stood off to the side and waited until she couldn't hear their voices anymore, and she waited another fifteen minutes before she dug out her flashlight, took a deep breath, and took the first step down.

She moved slowly out of fear that the men would backtrack to find her, or worse, that one or more had seen her and were waiting in the dark to surprise her. Back in the states she would have armed herself with at least a baton before getting into a situation like this, but on this trip, she hadn't prepared for any physical encounters.

Allie stepped off the bottom stair, hesitated for a moment, then walked along the corridor until she arrived at the junction. There, she shined her light on the ground, checking both directions for possible footprints. Neither option had enough dirt to leave full prints, and Allie was about to select a choice at random when she noticed a small pile of rocks. She checked around the corner and spotted a similar pile. A smile crossed her face.

"Good job, Drake," she whispered as she turned the corner and began searching for more piles.

Allie picked up her pace, confident in her ability to follow Drake's trail markers, but at one point she mistook a random pile of rubble for a cairn and headed down a wrong turn. When she got to the end of the corridor, she realized her mistake when she couldn't find another set of stones, and backtracked to where she needed to be.

She stopped when she heard voices. Allie couldn't make out the words, but based on the laughter and the tone she could tell that the Australians had found what they were looking for, and she knew she needed to slow them down, at least until she could find her friends. Allie ran back to the junction where she'd made her mistake and continued down the wrong corridor. Once at the end, she made a pile of rocks at the corners, exactly like Drake had done. When she finished, she returned to the correct turn and brushed away the pile. She moved down the corridor, stepped around the next turn, and turned off her flashlight.

"We're going to be rich," Allie heard Lachlan say. "I don't think we should turn these in. We should keep them for ourselves."

"What about the money?" Ethan asked.

"Good call. We turn them in, get the money, then take them back. It's a win-win for us."

"What do we do about the Americans?" Jack asked.

Lachlan laughed. "We leave them here. They'll be just another set of tourists who got lost in the Outback. Hopefully, the dingoes will get them."

"Did we miss a turn?" Ethan asked. "It feels like we should have turned by now."

"No. There are the rocks right there," Lachlan said. "Come on."

Allie waited until the voices disappeared and switched on her light and moved to the turn. She wanted to replace the pile, but instead created a line of six stones to guide the way, in case the Australians doubled back.

She broke into a jog, slowing at every corner she found to check her position and make sure she headed in the correct direction. When she came to the bridge, she slowed, but managed to cross it in a few strides before breaking back into a jog. She entered a room and in her flashlight beam she noticed a row of empty altars.

"Allie!"

Allie turned her flashlight toward the voice and spotted her friends tied together and sitting in a corner. She rushed to them, and within a few minutes, freed them of their bonds.

"What happened here?" Allie asked.

"We found the stone of the Rainbow Serpent!" Ingrid said.

"And the Australians found us," Drake groaned.

"You're injured?" Allie said, noticing his makeshift bandage.

"It's just a flesh wound," Drake said.

"Did they take the stone?" Allie asked.

"No. I hope not. I hid it before they got here," Ingrid said. "Come on, let's go see."

Allie handed her flashlight to Ingrid and together they crossed the bridge. Allie, Geneva, and Drake waited in the corridor while Ingrid retrieved her backpack.

"It's still here!" Ingrid said with delight.

"Can I look at it?" Allie asked.

"Let's get up top first," Ingrid said. "And we need to get away from those terrible men."

Allie smiled. "You won't have to worry about them. I moved some of Drake's piles so hopefully they're headed in the wrong direction. With luck, they won't be waiting for us at the top of the stairs."

"Nice one, Allie," Drake said.

Ingrid led the way, and when they found Allie's line of rocks that led to the correct way out, Drake took a moment to scatter the stones, and each time they turned a corner, he made a point to undo all the piles he'd made. After twenty minutes, they reached the stairs, climbed them, and found themselves in the late-afternoon sunshine.

"Do you think they made it out?" Ingrid asked.

"I doubt it," Drake said. "Without a map or a guide, they'll probably be wandering around in that labyrinth for a good long time."

"We'll stop by the ranger station and explain where they are on the way out. I'm sure the stewards of this place would like to know there's a series of hidden tunnels under there," Allie said.

"What should we do with this stone?" Ingrid asked.

The group stopped in a shady spot. Ingrid opened her backpack and retrieved it for Allie to see. As with Ingrid, the rock changed and started to glow different colors under Allie's touch.

"I've got an idea about what to do with this, too, but we'll need to hold on to it for a little while," Allie said.

"What do we do in the meantime?" Ingrid asked.

"We head back to the hotel. I don't know about you, but I need a nap and a shower."

* * *

"Is everything ready?" Ingrid asked as she entered the bedroom. She was fresh from the shower, one towel wrapped around her head, another around her body. She sat on the bed, removed the towel from her head, and ran a brush through her hair.

Allie nodded. "Yep. We only need to make the call and get it going."

"How's Drake doing this morning?"

Allie smiled. "I talked to Geneva a few minutes ago. He barely has a wound at all. Didn't even require stitches. They cleaned him up at the clinic, gave him a shot of antibiotics and a fresh bandage. The way he's carrying on, though, you'd think he'd lost his arm."

"That's Drake. Although he's had bad luck with injuries this trip."

"Yeah, well, better him than us." Allie started to laugh, but she didn't mean it.

"When are we doing this?" Ingrid asked.

"Well, my plan is to make the call and find out what time they want to meet, and then we're going to that diner down the street and getting some omelets for breakfast. After that, we'll take a leisurely drive over to the meeting place."

"You don't seem to be in any hurry," Ingrid said. She moved to the dresser and dug out her clothes for the day.

Allie shook her head. "Not really. I'm done chasing all over this country."

Ingrid nodded as she put on a pair of socks. "Okay. Make the call already. I'm starving."

Allie reached for the radio, which she'd brought in from the car.

"Hello? Come in someone?" she said.

She turned up the volume and listened to static for a few seconds.

"This is Aussie. Who is this?"

"It's Allie. We've done it. We found the final location and the grand prize. What do we do from here?"

"No way. What did you find? Um, to confirm it's the actual item."

"It's a round stone, about the same size as a soccer ball, has some kind of lights inside," Allie said.

"Did you say lights?" Aussie said.

"Yeah. Red, orange, purple. Lights."

"Hold on."

Allie held the radio for almost a minute before there was a short squelch.

"Congratulations. That's it. Tell me where you are and we'll come to you," Aussie said.

Allie gave him the coordinates.

"Great. We can be there in three hours. I need to round up the rest of the guys. They all want to be there."

Aussie cut out without saying goodbye.

"I guess that's that. Let's get the others and head out," Allie said.

Allie waited for Ingrid to finish dressing, then they rounded up Drake and Geneva and went for breakfast. Afterward, Ingrid drove them to the meeting coordinates, which was a dried-out lake an hour and a half northwest of Alice Springs.

Ingrid pulled off of the highway, followed a dirt road for a few miles, and stopped at a small parking area. It surprised them they were the only car in the area, especially considering they were already twenty minutes later than Allie thought they'd be.

"Allie where are the coordinates from here?" Geneva asked.

"Middle of the lake, about two hundred yards that way," Allie said, pointing to the southwest. "There is a large hill there, with four trees on top that are set in a perfect square, and in the middle of those trees is a large boulder. We should get a move on."

The four got out of the Jeep, and Ingrid grabbed her backpack and put it over her shoulders.

"You think this is going to work?" Ingrid asked.

"There's no reason why it wouldn't," Allie said. "Come on. Let's go find out."

The friends spread out and walked in a line down to the lake. The lakebed was bone dry and walking across it brought up poofs of fine sand with each step anyone took. They came to a rounded hill, climbed it, and found the trees exactly as Allie had described them. Since no one else was around, they all took seats in the shade and waited. As they did, the morning sun moved from its position in the east and settled straight overhead, removing most of the shade they'd enjoyed.

"How late are they?" Geneva asked, the impatience apparent in her voice.

Allie checked her phone. "A little over an hour."

They waited for another fifteen minutes in silence. Drake, bored with sitting around, stood and looked off into the distance.

"Hey," he said. "I think they're here."

"It's about time," Geneva said.

Drake watched as the four men marched down the bank and across the lake. "Um. Why would they be carrying shovels?"

"What?" Allie said. She pushed away from the tree she had her back against, and Drake helped her get to her feet.

Allie looked toward the shore and noticed the men coming at them. "What are the other two carrying?"

"I don't know. I can't make it out," Drake said.

The pair watched the men close the distance, and as they got to the bottom of the hill, Allie recognized the items. "A pickax, a shotgun, and two shovels. I don't think they're going to congratulate us on a job well done."

"What should we do?" Drake asked. "Make a run for it?"

Allie looked around and checked the landscape. "There's nowhere to run to. I think for now we need to play it straight. If you get a chance to disarm him, though, take it."

Drake nodded.

"Hey, fellas," Allie said as the men crested the hill.

"You have the artifact?" Aussie said.

"What, no g'day?" Allie teased.

Zeke removed the shotgun from his shoulder and chambered a round. "G'day. Where's the artifact?"

"It's in here," Ingrid said, holding up her backpack.

Aussie moved to her and snatched the bag from her hands and pushed Ingrid back to the ground when she tried to stand.

Drake made a motion to move toward her and stopped when Zeke stepped forward.

Aussie unzipped the backpack. He barely opened the bag when he saw a bright red glow come from inside. The red switched to orange. After a few seconds, it switched again to yellow. Aussie closed the backpack and slid it on. "Let's go for a walk."

Zeke gestured with his shotgun toward the lake, so the group ambled in that direction. Once they left the hill, Aussie led them farther from shore.

"That's far enough," Aussie said.

Jake, Zeke, and Ben dropped the shovels and pickax at Drake's feet.

"You know what to do," Aussie growled.

Drake's brow furrowed, then he softened, bent over, and retrieved the pickax. He moved a couple of feet away, swung and took a chunk out of the lake floor. Once he got a good-sized hole going, Geneva and Allie stepped in with shovels to clear away dirt while Ingrid moved larger rocks by hand.

The group worked for just over an hour, and the hole grew wider and deeper, until it was eventually hip-high on Drake.

"That's enough," Aussie said. "Everyone get in."

"No," Drake said. "No way."

"Get in. I won't tell you again."

Drake, still holding the pickax, raised it to chest level and took a step toward Aussie. In return, Zeke stepped toward Drake and leveled the shotgun at his chest.

"Drop it," Zeke warned.

Drake glared at Zeke, then he smiled.

"What's so funny?" Zeke asked.

Before Drake could answer, Zeke sensed motion from his left and turned just in time to see Allie swinging her shovel at him. Zeke raised an arm to block the blow, and it caught him in the ribs. He stumbled back a few paces and fell, releasing the shotgun. It skittered across the lake bed, then dropped into the hole.

The second Drake saw Allie swing the shovel, he swung the ax straight down and drove the tip of the ax right through Aussie's shoe, pinning his foot to the ground. Aussie screamed immediately and dropped to one knee. While he tried to wrest the pickax from the ground, Drake punched him in the jaw. Aussie's eyes rolled up in his head, and he fell to the ground, unconscious.

"Get the gun!" Drake yelled.

Geneva, Ingrid, Ben, and Jake seemed mesmerized by the events that happened just seconds earlier, but Drake's order spurred Geneva and Ben into action. They were equidistant from the hole, and both jumped in right away. Geneva was a fraction of a second faster and had her hands on the barrel when Ben pulled her hair back and punched her in the face. Geneva fell, and Ben ripped the gun out from under her prone body.

Ingrid had taken a single step toward the hole when Jake moved in front of her and brandished his knife. The overhead sun glinted off the blade, and Ingrid began quickly backing away from him.

Ben looked down and saw Geneva was still out cold. Since she was no longer a threat, he climbed out of the hole and fired a shot into the air.

"Everyone freeze!" he yelled. "Next one of you to move gets a chest full of lead."

Ingrid stopped moving. Jake caught up with her, stepped behind her, and pulled her hair back, turning her face to the sky. He positioned his knife to her neck and, using her hair like a horse's reins, moved her to the hole. When they got to the edge, he stopped, removed the knife, and pushed her in. Ingrid let out a cry as she fell the few feet, and although she attempted to avoid Geneva's body, she caught Geneva's foot in her stomach, which knocked the breath from her lungs.

Ben gestured with the gun for Drake and Allie to move to the hole. They had an unspoken moment between them, but complied.

As soon as Allie saw Geneva's condition, she bent over and assessed her friends' injuries. Geneva's nose bled profusely, so Allie rolled her onto her side so she wouldn't choke on the blood. She moved Geneva's hair away from her face and softly whispered her name. After a few calls, Geneva's eyes opened.

"Allie?"

"I'm here."

"Am I dead?"

Allie smiled, despite the question and circumstances. "Not yet, honey. Do you think you can sit up?"

Geneva struggled at first, so Allie grabbed Geneva's shoulders and gently helped her sit.

"Lean your head forward, and breathe through your mouth, okay?" Allie said.

"Mmm-kay," Geneva said as she took Allie's advice.

"You, get back up here and check on Aussie," Ben ordered.

Drake gave Allie a boost from the hole and she moved to Aussie's side.

"Well?" Ben asked. "How is he?"

"He's unconscious, as you can see. As far as the foot wound, it's hard to tell."

"Pull out the ax and look at it then," Ben said.

Allie shook her head. "Not a good idea without a well-stocked first aid kit. That ax may be the only thing keeping him from bleeding to death."

"You're saying there's nothing you can do?" Ben asked.

"No," Allie said. "Not without the proper equipment. You know how it is out here. He might not even make it back to Alice Springs."

"Okay. That just means that you're expendable then."

Ben raised the rifle and aimed it at Allie's chest.

Allie took a deep breath and held it, all the while staring into Ben's eyes.

Ben's muscles tensed, then he stopped moving. Ben blinked twice, then fell over onto his back.

Allie watched as a bright red spot expanded over his left shoulder. She glanced toward the shore and saw a group of Aboriginal rangers running in her direction.

"Better late than never," Allie mumbled to herself.

CHAPTER TWENTY-ONE

"You made it!" Lenah said, jumping from her bench. She moved to the door before Allie could open it, and hugged the four people waiting to get in. "I hope you don't mind, but Uncle Jarli invited a few close friends over."

Lenah opened the door and held it while the friends entered.

The center was awash in people, all standing shoulder to shoulder, and although the building was loud with echoing voices and conversations, silence descended as Lenah stepped in behind Ingrid and shut the door behind her.

"Make way to the stage," Lenah shouted.

The crowd parted, and the group walked to the front of the room and climbed the stairs to the raised stage. Uncle Jarli waited at center stage, surrounded by six other tribal elders. Allie joined them first, and Uncle Jarli introduced her to the elders, then did the same with Geneva, Ingrid, and Drake.

Once Uncle Jarli got through the elders, he introduced the group to the crowd, and as each of the embarrassed Americans stepped forward when their name was called, they got a polite round of applause from the packed room. At his insistence, Allie and Ingrid told their story about what brought them to Australia, and their challenge to find what they assumed at first was a geocache, but what turned out to be a quest to find the stone of the Rainbow Serpent. As they went through their adventure, Uncle Jarli would ask questions.

"I'm curious," Uncle Jarli asked as Allie got closer to the end of the tale. "How did you convince them that you had the stone?"

Allie smiled. "A little ingenuity from Drake and a trip to the hardware store. Ingrid?"

Ingrid pulled her backpack from her shoulders, unzipped it, and set on the lectern what looked like one of the geodes. She waved a hand, and like magic, the geode glowed with red lights, then orange, and they cycled through all seven colors of the rainbow and started again at red.

"This is the stone?" Uncle Jarli asked, stepped up to take a closer look.

"No," Ingrid said. "This is a soccer ball embedded with programmable LED lights and covered with quick drying cement and coated with dirt from the parking lot of our hotel."

"And this fooled your captors?" Uncle Jarli asked. "This looks like you made it as a part of a school project." A majority of the crowd laughed at the comment.

"I know," Ingrid said. "But we were hoping that they wouldn't take a close look at it and they'd want to get on the move. What we didn't count on was them wanting to shoot and bury us at the lake."

"How did you escape death?" Uncle Jarli asked. He grinned and stepped away from the microphone. He already knew the story, and this was his favorite part.

"You want to take this one?" Ingrid asked Allie.

"I suppose."

Ingrid stepped away from the lectern and let Allie take her place.

"We had an arrangement with the rangers that we would

lure the bad guys out to the lake, and the rangers would pick them up on the way out. Fortunately, they got nervous when it took them so long to show up, so they came in after us," Allie explained. "In the end, the rangers saved our hides, and we are indebted to them."

Allie's comments got another round of applause from the crowd. There were several rangers in attendance, and they got plenty of kudos. Allie waved her arms to quiet the room.

"Before we go, we'd like to make a presentation. Uncle Jarli, please step forward."

Drake smiled at Uncle Jarli and patted him on the back as he passed. Ingrid moved to the podium and replaced her backpack with a large box.

Allie cleared her throat and put her hand on his arm. "Uncle Jarli, a lot of people were looking for this, and I'm sure if we could find it, others eventually would too. Whether this is a mystical item or not, it belongs to you and your people. You are the stewards of the land, so this belongs to you."

Allie stepped backward in line with her friends.

Uncle Jarli removed the lid from the box, looked into it, and grinned. He reached in and held over his head for all of his people to see the legendary stone of the Rainbow Serpent.

* * *

"What time does the plane leave?" Drake asked.

Allie checked her phone. "We've got to be at the airport in just over four hours, so we have plenty of time to find this cache."

"I hate rock pile caches," Geneva said as she picked up another palm-sized rock, turned it over, and set it back down.

"Me too," Ingrid said. She'd long given up searching in the rock pile and was leaning up against their rental car.

"Did Lenah ever call you?" Geneva said.

"She did this morning. The authorities arrested our

Australian friends for a variety of charges, including kidnapping and attempted murder. They finally found the Germans. They'd been run off the road, and all four of them will be in the hospital for at least a week." Allie stopped talking when she saw an odd-looking rock. She turned it over and discovered she'd found just another rock and not the geocache. "It turns out that our hosts hired those guys who followed us under Uluru. They and the other American team are actually professional treasure hunters."

"I thought it was something like that," Ingrid said. "Did they get arrested, too?"

Allie nodded. "Again, tying you up and leaving you for dead wasn't a good plan on their part."

"I wonder how long it took them to get out of the mountain," Geneva said.

"Two days," Allie said. "Once the batteries in their flashlights died, they had no chance to find their own way out and had to be rescued."

"I guess that wraps up all the loose ends, then," Geneva said.

"Nope. There's still one," Drake said.

"What's that?"

Drake removed his hat and scratched his head. "Where is this stupid geocache?"

ABOUT THE AUTHOR

Dan DeKoning was born and raised in Milwaukee, Wisconsin, and currently lives in Knoxville, Tennessee with his wife and their cats.

He is a storyteller and poet who loves to write in a variety of genres and themes. He is also a voracious reader who loves to read anything he can get his hands on.

When he's not writing, you can find him hunting for treasures in used bookstores, or out exploring the planet, or geocaching, or searching for adventures and stories to tell.

BIBLIOGRAPHY

<u>Fiction</u>
Déjà Vu
The Haunting of Hyacinth House
How Deep the Darkness
Baker's Crossing
How Bright the Light

<u>Geocaching Mystery Series</u>
The Cacheland Conspiracy
The Quincy Bay Quandary
The Secret of the Seven Valleys
The Geocaching Mystery Omnibus – Volume 1

<u>Codi Cassidy Cozy Mystery Series</u>
Acoustics and Alibis
Ballads and Bloodshed
Codas and Calibers
Codi Cassidy Omnibus – Volume 1

<u>Poetry Collections</u>
Lost and Found
Random Thoughts